Spetsnaz hunting party

A crackle of autofire rang out, and bullets shredded the foliage only a few feet away. "Get under cover," Manning yelled. Dropped to one knee, he raised the SA-80 smoothly to his shoulder. He aimed and fired, sending a man sprawling facedown in the long grass. High in the trees the monkeys screeched in alarm, and the sky was alive with startled birds.

Crawling backward, he caught up with Grimaldi and Roskov as a hail of bullets slammed into the dense thickets near them. "Let's move. We have to try and lose them."

But after some ten minutes of trying to slip through the human net, Manning said, "We're not going to get through. And there's no way to outshoot this bunch. There are too many of them."

The enemy troops began to close in, and the three raised their hands as the first of the Russian Spetsnaz emerged from the undergrowth. They formed a grim circle around the trio, their AK-47 assault rifles unwaveringly trained on the captives.

Mack Bolan's
PHOENIX FORCE.

PHOENIX FORCE®

GAR WILSON

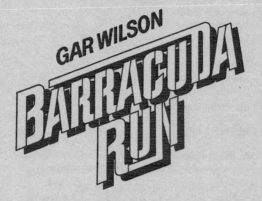

BARRACUDA RUN

A GOLD EAGLE BOOK FROM
WORLDWIDE®

TORONTO · NEW YORK · LONDON · PARIS
AMSTERDAM · STOCKHOLM · HAMBURG
ATHENS · MILAN · TOKYO · SYDNEY

First edition July 1990

ISBN 0-373-61348-2

Special thanks and acknowledgment to
Michael Linaker for his contribution to this work.

Printed in U.S.A.

PROLOGUE

Major Yuri Grigorevich Tchenko stormed onto the bridge of the *Chekov*. Small in stature but with a well-knit build, he resembled a shrewd sleek weasel. Or perhaps a Russian sable—dark haired, quick and fierce. His sharp features were now aggressively pointed at the captain of the Soviet aircraft carrier. Tchenko had to tilt his head upward to glare at the six-footer from Vladivostok. Born and raised in Moscow, Tchenko considered anyone, even a Soviet citizen, from anywhere outside the capital of the USSR to be a lesser life form.

"I have been informed Ilya Roskov and Barracuda have disappeared, Captain," Tchenko declared. "What do you have to say about this?"

Captain Zimin's wide face remained as stoic as stone. He resented Tchenko's presence on his vessel. Security officers aboard Soviet warships are usually GRU, military Intelligence. The GRU was bad enough, but Tchenko was KGB. The all-powerful Committee for State Security was feared and hated by regular Soviet military. The captain did not know why the KGB was involved, but he did not like it.

Finally he offered a slight smile and said, "Well, as I see it, we appear to be minus one pilot and plane."

Tchenko forced himself to remain calm. "I am aware of that. What I need to know is why."

"Perhaps an accident or pilot error. The plane may have come down in the water."

"Or maybe Roskov has defected," Tchenko suggested, "taking Barracuda with him."

The captain shrugged. "I suppose it could be."

"It is your job to know."

"No, Major Tchenko, it is your job to be aware of such things. Let us get our positions right. I command the ship and crew. Your function is to monitor their thoughts and state of mind. Don't try and confuse me with your KGB rhetoric. As far as I and my staff are concerned, Lieutenant Roskov behaved perfectly normally this morning. I spoke to him myself only fifteen minutes before he took off. There were certainly no indications of abnormal behavior then. Nothing to suggest he was considering anything other than a normal test flight. If there had been any suspicions, the flight would have been canceled."

Tchenko considered his position. He was aware that the captain was no fool. The man had stated his position with clarity, and as much as he would have liked, Tchenko could not put any blame on him. So it was down to him.

"Do you have the flight plan?" he asked.

Zimin nodded. He raised a hand to one of his aides, who passed across a sheet of paper. The captain eased himself from the seat and walked across to the chart table.

"We are here," he indicated. "Roskov was to have taken Barracuda northeast, then to the south. He would then have turned north on his return run. He was tracked northeast at this point. And then he changed course completely and flew directly south well before he should have. We tracked him as far as here before he left the radar screens."

"Have you continued to sweep the area?"

"Of course. We are still checking."

"How could he vanish so easily?"

"Remember that Barracuda is an advanced version of the MiG-27. One of its inbuilt features is the capacity to avoid radar detection. That is why it is fitted with TFR, Terrain-Following Radar, which allows it to fly almost at ground or sea level in order to remain undetectable. Remember also that Roskov is an excellent pilot. He has superb control over his craft. If you put such a man into a plane like Barracuda, you have a formidable combination."

"Damn!" Tchenko snapped. He turned to stare across the seemingly endless spread of the placid ocean. "Until such time when we obtain evidence to the contrary," he said, "we will assume that Lieutenant Roskov has chosen to defect with Barracuda. Working on that premise, we must next consider where he might be going."

"The most obvious destination would be the United States," Zimin remarked. "However, Roskov does not have enough fuel to carry him so far. I'd say he has a couple of choices. Either he lands the plane somewhere on the South American continent, or he will rendezvous with an American aircraft carrier for refueling or concealment."

Tchenko studied the chart again, tracing Barracuda's new flight path with a stubby finger.

"If he maintains this course, it would appear that the U.S.A. could be his destination."

Suddenly the KGB man tapped the chart authoritatively. "Here," he said. "We may still have a chance of tracking him."

Zimin glanced at the point Tchenko was indicating and saw it was the waters near the coastline of Guatemala.

"Come with me," Tchenko said, and, intrigued, Zimin followed him from the bridge.

Tchenko made directly for the radio room, with the captain close behind. With his usual disregard for any kind of protocol, the KGB man strode into the radio room and up to the first of the radio operators.

"You," Tchenko snapped, drawing the operator's attention.

The operator glanced at the captain, who nodded quickly, silently informing the man to do whatever Tchenko told him. The captain of the carrier didn't like Tchenko's methods, but he knew enough not to challenge him. It wasn't a wise thing to go around deliberately upsetting members of the KGB. They were notorious for their vindictiveness and a singular lack of any sense of humor.

"I want you to get this frequency," Tchenko said, scribbling some figures on the radio operator's message pad.

The operator adjusted his headphones and leaned forward as he worked the frequency changes on his set. He finally looked up at Tchenko. "I have the frequency," he said.

"Good. Now make contact."

"What reference?" asked the radio operator.

"The *Pushkin*," the KGB man told him, and once again the radio operator bent to his task.

"I presume the *Pushkin* is one of our vessels?" the captain ventured.

Tchenko saw no reason why the captain should not know. He reasoned that if he extended this courtesy to the man, he might be satisfied.

"Yes," he said. "The *Pushkin* is one of our Lentra Class AGI Intelligence vessels."

The Lentra Class vessels were in fact floating information-gatherers. Their function was to pick up and monitor any and all kinds of information that might conceivably be of use to the Soviet machine. Equipped with the latest in electronic listening and recording devices, radar and sonar, tracking, the vessels—camouflaged as merchant ships—plied their secret trade wherever the Kremlin taskmasters sent them.

"You think it might be able to pick up Barracuda?" the captain asked.

"It's worth the attempt," Tchenko said. "If Roskov is flying toward the destination we talked about, then he may pass within the *Pushkin*'s radar sweep. The Lentra Class vessels are fitted with the most powerful radar systems we have, capable of great range. The *Pushkin* is operating along the Pacific coastline of Guatemala. That could easily be Roskov's flight path. We may not be able to stop him, but at least we may be able to track him. I'm certain he will have to refuel before he can reach the United States. If we could identify where he might do that, then possibly we can get some of our people in to make sure he does not go any farther."

Zimin couldn't fault Tchenko's logic. The KGB man certainly knew his business, but that was not surprising. The KGB were a race apart. They functioned under a great cloak of secrecy, and their methods were mysterious to anyone beyond that enveloping cloak. One thing had to be admitted about them: they were totally professional in their approach to their work. They were absolutely loyal to the state and its creed. And they were fanatical in their pursuit of anyone daring to betray the Marxist way of life.

The captain felt no bitterness toward Ilya Roskov. The young pilot had obviously decided to change his way of life, opting for the greater possibilities and freedom of the United States—something the captain had thought about more than once in his long life— and the captain wished him well. He did not, however, think much of Roskov's chances. Especially now that he had Tchenko on his trail.

"I have the *Pushkin* for you, Comrade Tchenko," the radio operator said.

Tchenko put on a headset and picked up a microphone. "I wish to speak to Major Barishnov. Send someone for him this minute. Say that Tchenko of the KGB wishes to speak with him." Tchenko stared into space while he waited for the man named Barishnov to come to the radio.

"Barishnov? This is Yuri. Yes, it's good to hear your voice. We have a slight problem which I am sure you will be able to help us with."

Tchenko detailed the events of Roskov's flight and the possibility that he might be making a run for the United States. He explained that he needed to obtain some information on Barracuda's whereabouts and that all of the *Pushkin*'s electronic equipment be put to use.

"Thank you, Barishnov. Your cooperation will not go unheeded. Come up with some solid information, and I can guarantee your next visit to Moscow will be well received. You will call me back the moment you have anything of significance to report? Good. I look forward to hearing from you."

Tchenko tossed microphone and headset back on the radio console.

"Keep this frequency open," he ordered the operator. "Our contact with the *Pushkin* must be maintained without a break. Understand?"

"Yes, Comrade Tchenko."

The KGB man turned to the captain. "I feel like a drink. Will you join me?"

The captain nodded, deciding to play along with the obnoxious KGB operative.

"If anything comes through, I want to know immediately," Tchenko said to the radio operator. "Immediately!"

Tchenko followed the captain out of the radio room. "Now all we can do is wait," he said, almost showing his teeth in a cold smile.

Within the hour, Tchenko had his call from the *Pushkin*, and with it the opportunity to recover both Roskov and Barracuda had been thrust into his hands.

1

Two hundred feet below Dragon Slayer, the Pacific Ocean sparkled in the midday sunlight. Sitting easily at the controls of the Stony Man combat helicopter, Jack Grimaldi glanced at his passenger.

"What do you think, Gary?" he asked.

Gary Manning, the Canadian member of Phoenix Force, the ultrasecret commando team, merely nodded his head.

"Is that 'yes she's okay,' or 'yes you're thinking about it'?"

Manning dragged himself back to the present. It had been so relaxing in the pressurized cabin of Dragon Slayer, shut off from the real world beyond the sealed canopy, that Manning had drifted, allowing himself to bring to mind the couple of weeks he'd spent in Germany recently, in between missions, with the beautiful Karen Hoffe. He had met Karen some months back, during a Phoenix Force mission in Germany, and both he and the stunning lady police officer had experienced a mutual attraction. It was one of those instant relationships, and despite the difficulties thrown up by both their jobs, Manning and Karen were determined to keep their feelings alive. After the mission in Germany had been completed, Manning had managed to grab a few days with Karen. A couple of months had gone by before he was able to get another break and hop a plane to Frankfurt, where Karen was based. The time had flown by, but the couple had managed to get away on their own, enjoying every minute of each other's company.

Now Manning was back in harness—though this particular mission was a peaceful one. Since David McCarter, the Phoenix Force unit pilot, had not arrived in time to assist Grimaldi in assessing the performance of Dragon Slayer, the Canadian pro had volunteered for the job. Half the reason Manning had done it was to get McCarter's goat. The British commando never missed an opportunity to get on Manning's nerves, so the Canadian tried to return the favor as often as possible. This was really a good-natured feud they conducted between combat assignments, and they both actually enjoyed the one-upmanship, although neither would have admitted it.

However, Manning was surprised to discover he genuinely enjoyed flying Dragon Slayer. The trials were being conducted over the Pacific from a temporary HQ on the U.S. Navy aircraft carrier *Anaconda* which was cruising international waters near Mexico's Gulf of Tehuantepec. Grimaldi and Manning had been flying the area for the past three days, putting the sleek black combat craft through its paces.

The technicians had been working on Dragon Slayer over a number of weeks, upgrading the power of the turbo-boosting engine and improving the handling qualities. Dragon Slayer's electrically operated rotary cannon had also been improved. Its already awesome rate of fire had been increased. With a new sighting and firing system, all coupled to the on-board computer, Dragon Slayer's firepower was something to see.

The combat chopper, which had proved itself on a number of Stony Man missions, already boasted rocket pods that could carry a mixture of loads—including heat-seeking missiles—under each stub-wing. It had electro-optical sensors on each wingtip to aid target location, and coupled to these was an air-data probe that measured airspeed, drift and angle of approach, feeding it to the on-board computer, which would then calculate the correct firing coordinates. Dragon Slayer carried state-of-the-art communication and tracking equipment. The computer also contained the facility of being able to work out a required course, via the map program included in its data base.

During the trials Grimaldi had pushed Dragon Slayer to the limit, throwing the combat machine through the sky in high-speed turns and dives, putting the chopper into a level throttle-wide run that took it to full speed. He tested the fearsome rotary cannon on dummy targets put up by the carrier, blasting the objects almost out of existence.

During the flights Grimaldi took time to pass some of his flying experience to Manning. The Canadian had done a little preliminary training, but all that went out of the window when he came under the eye of the master. Grimaldi made the learning easy. He had a laid-back manner that relaxed his pupil and kept him that way, and no matter what mistakes were made, Grimaldi passed them over by using them to explain how the particular maneuver should have been carried out. With no kind of stress to badger him, Manning picked up the basics very quickly. He was by nature a man able to master complicated techniques with comparative ease, and the complexities of handling a helicopter didn't present him with any overt problems. He was pleased to learn because he was well aware of the requirements placed on Phoenix Force when they were in the field. Circumstances could change very rapidly, and the need to operate some piece of hardware often arose out of the blue. Although Manning was the team's explosives expert, as well as the crack sniper, due to his skill at long-range pinpoint shooting, he acknowledged that it was a necessary thing to be able to turn his hand to other combat skills. He also enjoyed flying for the sheer thrill of being able to control a machine like Dragon Slayer and send it howling across the sky. The experience was nothing less than exhilarating.

Right at the moment when Jack Grimaldi had spoken to him, Manning had opted out for a short time, drifting and daydreaming, letting his thoughts flow freely.

He sat forward, turning to look at Grimaldi. The flyer grinned at the expression on Manning's face.

"Hey, sorry, pal," Grimaldi apologized. "I didn't realize you were gone."

Manning rubbed a hand across his face, shaking his head to clear away the muzziness. "The going was fine," the Canadian said. "It was the coming back that caused the problem."

"No sweat," Grimaldi remarked.

"You asked me something?" Manning said.

"Just what you thought of the lady's performance."

"Great. She's performing one hundred percent. There anything left to check?"

"No. We've covered everything the tech boys asked us to. I figure we can head home tomorrow."

"You're the boss," Manning said.

The radio speaker hissed briefly before a voice came through. "Dragon Slayer, this is Base One. Do you acknowledge? Over."

Manning spoke into his throat mike. "Base One from Dragon Slayer. Receiving you clear. Over."

"Priority, Dragon Slayer. Return to Base One immediately. Over."

"Base One from Dragon Slayer. We acknowledge your instruction and are returning to base. Over and out."

"Now, what the heck is that all about?" Grimaldi asked.

Manning didn't know specifically, but he was certain of one thing—there was trouble looming on the horizon, and he had a sneaking feeling it was heading in their direction.

"Let's get back to mother and find out," he suggested.

Grimaldi nodded, touching the controls, and sent Dragon Slayer in a descending curve toward the glittering Pacific below. He leveled out at fifty feet, opening the powerful engine. The sleek black shape of the helicopter flashed above the gentle swell of the ocean as it sped toward the huge gray bulk of the *Anaconda*.

Ten minutes later Manning and Grimaldi were shown into a cabin whose furnishings were a table and a few chairs. On the table was a telephone. The moment the door closed Manning picked up the receiver.

"Having a nice time down there?" asked a voice from the earpiece. It was electronically distorted and had the quality of a robot in a 1950 sci-fi film.

"We were until a minute ago," Manning said into the mouthpiece. "I figure this is no social call. Do we have a problem?"

"Only a small one," the robot voice promised.

"That's a new one," the Canadian replied with a chuckle.

Although the voice was distorted to prevent identification by voiceprint or evaluation by stress analysis, Manning knew who the caller was. Hal Brognola, the Head of Operations at Stony Man, was the only one who would be calling him at sea, and the electrically scrambled voice confirmed that it had to be the Fed.

"By now the carrier has started to change course," Brognola explained. "As soon as we've finished talking, I want you and your flyboy friend back in the air."

"Heading for where?"

"Guatemala," Brognola said.

"Gee," Manning said in mock amazement, although he was genuinely surprised. "That was easy. No codes or indirect answers that I have to look on the map and try to turn words backward to figure out what you mean?"

"We're not slacking off on security," the Fed assured him, "but this is sort of a rush job. It's important, but hopefully not particularly dangerous."

"I'm surprised you even called me," the Canadian commented, steadily more intrigued by the mission...if that was indeed what it was.

"There's a plane down a few miles inland from the Pacific coast in Guatemala. Engine trouble apparently. We need a rescue mission. A quick flight in so you two can take a look and get that jet bird airworthy again. Then out and back to the carrier."

"Sounds easy enough." Manning frowned. "Too easy. What's the catch?"

"The plane and the pilot are Russian," the Stony Man boss continued. "The plane is a state-of-the-art MiG fighter jet. Code-named 'Barracuda.' It's the most advanced new military toy to fly the not always friendly skies of the USSR. State Department already got the story, and so did a couple of clowns in Congress. That means it will be on the six o'clock news by tomorrow night. Security isn't too tight on this already, so you may as well know the pilot's name. He's Lieutenant Ilya Mikhailovich Roskov and he's defecting to the United States and bringing us Barracuda as a bargain."

"Sounds like the Belenko defection back in 1976," Manning remarked.

"You got a good memory," Brognola replied. "Yeah. Belenko's defection made a lot of people in the U.S. government happy, and it pissed off a lot of Russians. Of course, he had to land in Japan, and the Soviet government eventually got that MiG back. Japanese Kompei and the CIA got in and photographed everything to the smallest detail, and we learned a lot about the MiG-25 Foxbat fighters before the Soviets got their hands on it again. But the

MiG-25 is ancient news now. It's a horse and buggy compared to the Barracuda."

"And it's just a coincidence that we happen to be aboard the *Anaconda* when this happened?" Manning asked with a grin.

"As long as you fellows needed to do some test flying, there was no reason you shouldn't be handy," Brognola confirmed. "Nobody mentioned it to you earlier, because we couldn't be sure the defection would happen. Roskov may not have gotten the chance to make his run. If he did, he was supposed to rendezvous with the *Anaconda*. Apparently he had to go off course for some reason."

"Maybe that's because half the Soviet navy is after him by now," Manning said with a groan. "That's more than a small problem."

"He took off from a Soviet carrier over three hundred miles from your position," the Fed explained. "He was on a routine test flight and made the dodge for freedom. Barracuda is equipped to fly under radar, so he probably got out of range before they knew which way he went. It should take them a while before they can lock in on him, but the Russians will have a general idea which direction he went. Even if they figure it out, they'll be reluctant to head inland to Guatemala."

"You hope," Manning muttered.

"Don't we all," Brognola remarked. "We have to make the most of what time we've got. Got to move quick without arousing too much suspicion from the locals. There are Marxist terrorists running around in the general area Roskov went down. Revolutionary Armed Forces, or the FAR. Stands for the Fuerzas

Armadas Revolucionario. It's hard to tell how FAR might react if they get wind of this."

"It's not too hard to figure out which side they'll be on if they suspect Roskov is trying to defect from the Soviets to join us American capitalist imperialist pigs," Manning said with a sigh. "I guess the faster we move, the better our chances. Do we have a definite fix on Roskov's location?"

"Yeah," the Fed confirmed. "Check with Captain Garner. Roskov gave us detailed coordinates. Feed them into the computer, and it should give you precise information about his fix."

Manning understood that the computer Brognola referred to was the one aboard Dragon Slayer.

"Okay," Brognola continued. "If it comes down to a crunch and you can't get the MiG back in the air, destroy Barracuda and lift Roskov out with you. He's gone through some top-level training in technical engineering as well as flying the jet. The information in Roskov's head is worth even more than the plane itself. Still, we're greedy and we'd like to have both, if possible."

"We'll give it our best shot," Manning promised.

"Good luck and be as careful as the job allows," Brognola urged before he ended transmission.

Manning turned to Grimaldi. "You get most of that?"

"Enough to know this isn't gonna be a milk run anymore," the pilot answered. "Do you feel like filling me in on the details?"

"Not really," Manning admitted, but he gave Grimaldi a quick rundown on the assignment. There was little time to spare, and they had to see the captain before they left in Dragon Slayer once more.

2

Grimaldi pointed to the map displayed on the on-board computer screen. ''That's our destination,'' he said.

The detailed map section showed the Pacific coastline of Guatemala. Coordinates fed into the computer had resulted in a flickering spot of light on the map; this marker represented Barracuda's resting place.

As Dragon Slayer sped toward the Guatemalan coast, in the seat next to Jack Grimaldi, Manning quietly checked his weapons.

Officially it was to be a soft probe, without prejudice. A simple rescue mission that would hopefully be over in a couple of hours.

Despite the peaceful intent of their mission, Manning saw no reason why they should not go in prepared.

The Canadian warrior slipped on his leather shoulder rig, with the Walther P-5, 9 mm autopistol nestled in the holster. With that in place he turned his attention to his SA80 rifle—the newest weapon in his personal arsenal—which he used as well as his FAL assault rifle. The British SA80, officially adopted by that country's armed forces, had served Manning well on a number of missions, and he had familiarized himself thoroughly with its capabilities. Manning fed in a magazine of 5.56 mm cartridges, then placed the loaded weapon in one of the gunracks positioned beside the seat.

"Let's hope you don't need that thing," Grimaldi said through his throat mike.

"Amen to that," Manning replied.

Grimaldi was armed with a 9 mm Uzi and a Colt .45 automatic.

Dragon Slayer, under Grimaldi's expert guidance, began a long, graceful descent as the Guatemalan coast appeared below them. The Stony Man flyer put the combat helicopter on a low run, skimming the waves of the blue Pacific. They were following as closely as they were able the same course Barracuda had taken on its emergency flight.

Ahead they could see the shoreline and the dense spread of the green forest, rising and falling with the undulations of the land.

"This Roskov must be one hell of a pilot," Manning said, voicing his thoughts. "Landing a supersonic jet fighter in that mess."

"You said it, pal," Grimaldi agreed. "This is one Russian I'm looking forward to meeting. He isn't good—he's great."

Manning, monitoring the blip on the computer screen, advised the flyer on any changes that showed. Overlaid on the screen were coordinates and distances.

"According to baby, we have five miles to go, Jack. Keep on this heading."

Grimaldi nodded. He was already climbing slightly as the coastline rushed to meet them. He kept the chopper just above tree height, losing a little speed as they began the final run in to their touchdown.

Glancing at his watch, Manning saw that it was almost two hours to the minute since they had taken off from the *Anaconda*. The carrier itself was cruising in their general direction, waiting for the eventual arrival of the Russian plane and its defecting pilot.

Manning was getting a flicker of unease in his stomach. It was that faint but unsettling sensation that preceded genuine concern over the way things were shaping up. The Canadian was not a superstitious man. He preferred to base his decisions on practical evidence or plain and simple gut feeling, the kind of gut feeling that a seasoned warrior developed over the years. The sort that warned of possible problems ahead. It had nothing to do with precognition or any mumbo jumbo. Manning simply felt that he and Grimaldi might find themselves flying right into the middle of something more than just a quick search-and-rescue situation. He hoped he was wrong. He hoped he was just being overcautious.

Even so, he was glad he and Grimaldi were armed and that Dragon Slayer was equipped with enough firepower to handle most emergencies.

The blip on the screen was emphasized by an audible warning. It was a low, steady signal that indicated the target area was extremely close. The tone would stay until it was manually switched off. It would, however, fade if Grimaldi happened to fly off course by a wide margin.

Throttling back even more, Grimaldi flew Dragon Slayer slowly above the seemingly impenetrable green canopy of the Guatemalan jungle. "Up ahead," the flyer said.

Manning stared through the canopy and saw the break in the greenery. A wide stretch of treeless earth, covered with waving grass and ferns, ran on for almost a quarter of a mile. To one side was a winding stream, and at the far end was a steep slope that lost itself in the ever-present mass of the jungle.

Grimaldi let Dragon Slayer sink to the ground, hovering a few feet above it. The chopper's rotor wash sent the grass and ferns swaying, turning the area into a sea of shimmering green waves.

"I don't see any plane," Manning said.

Grimaldi cut the power the moment Dragon Slayer touched the ground.

"Roskov isn't about to advertise the fact he's here, Gary. He'll have Barracuda in as close to the trees as he could get and camouflaged by now."

"That's what I hate about you flyboys," Manning joked. "You're all a bunch of smart asses."

"Just part of the charm and mystery," Grimaldi replied.

He leaned forward to activate Dragon Slayer's weapons system. From his seat he could operate the rotary cannon and even launch one of the collection of missiles at his disposal.

Manning slipped off his headset and picked up the SA8O, cocking the weapon as he unlatched his cabin hatch in preparation to leave the helicopter.

"Watch my back," the Phoenix commando said.

Grimaldi nodded. "It's covered," he acknowledged.

As his feet touched the ground, Manning felt the steamy heat of the day slap him in the face. The humid air clung to him. Now that he was out of the pressurized comfort of Dragon Slayer, Manning realized how it isolated its passengers. His ears were assailed by the noise of the jungle's occupants. The distant screech and chatter of birds, mainly the brightly colored parrots that dominate the Guatemalan forests, rose and fell. Occasionally the feathered creatures would burst into view, leaping up from the tree branches to swoop across the sky before plunging back into the dense greenery. Manning even spotted a few monkeys capering about wildly in the high branches.

Grimaldi's voice reached him from the chopper.

"That Russian bird is straight ahead, Gary. Far end of the clearing. Roskov has hidden it well. If you look close, you can see some of the tracks his landing gear made when it touched down. Lucky for him the long grass sprang back up again and concealed the worst."

Manning raised a silent hand in thanks and started off across the open space. His gaze was fixed on the distant end of the clearing, and as he shifted his line of vision back and forth, he began to pick out the more rigid shape of the greenery ahead of him. After a while he was able to identify the basic outline of the concealed jet.

A sudden rush of sound drew his attention, and Manning swiveled around as the muzzle of his SA80 tracked the source. It was only a bird with brilliant plumage, bursting from a thick clump of ferns and soaring skyward.

Turning back, Manning continued his walk across the clearing. He halted yards from the concealed aircraft. Now he could see the dull gleam of its aluminum skin through the tangle of chopped branches and ferns covering it in a careful latticework. Obviously the Soviet training machine taught its pupils well in the art of camouflage.

Manning lowered the muzzle of the SA8O to indicate that he was not making any threat.

"Lieutenant Ilya Roskov," he said. "Please show yourself. I am a representative of the United States government, sent to assist in getting your aircraft repaired so you may continue your flight to rendezvous with the USS *Anaconda*."

Silence greeted Manning's declaration. He remained where he was, waiting, allowing the Russian his moment of caution.

A faint rustling to Manning's right indicated a response. The thick foliage parted, and a tall young man clad in a high-altitude flying suit stepped into view. He held a Makarov 9 mm automatic pistol in his right hand, the muzzle pointed steadily at Manning.

"How quickly will we be able to get away from here?" the Russian asked in flawless English.

"That all depends on what we find," Manning said. "I'm Jackson, by the way."

Roskov managed a quick smile. "Nice to meet you, Mr. Jackson."

"I have a colleague in the helicopter," Manning explained. "He's an experienced flyer. He'll find out what's wrong with this Barracuda."

Roskov lowered the Makarov. He suddenly looked very tired and much younger than his years. "Then call him over, please," he said.

Manning turned and waved Grimaldi in. The Stony Man flyer fired up Dragon Slayer and lifted the combat chopper a couple of feet off the ground, cruising slowly across the clearing. He put the machine down as close as he could get to the concealed Russian jet, cut the power and climbed out.

"Lieutenant Roskov, this is Mr. Monk."

Grimaldi nodded, shrewdly eyeing the young Soviet pilot for a moment. Then he grinned with open admiration. "Roskov, that was one hell of a landing you made. I'd like to shake your hand."

The Russian stared at the outstretched hand for a moment, then he put out his own.

"Might be a little premature," Manning said, "but welcome to America."

"That is what I have been waiting to hear someone say," Roskov replied, beaming widely. "Thank you, my friends."

"Okay, Roskov," Grimaldi said, "let's go take a look at this bird of yours and see what's made her sick."

Grimaldi and Roskov disappeared beneath the canopy shielding Barracuda, leaving Manning to stand watch. He moved out and wandered across to Dragon Slayer. Standing by the open hatch, he listened to the clicks and creaks of Dragon Slayer's motor cooling. Metal pinged musically as it contracted. The smell of hot metal merged with the tang of decay from the overripe vegetation.

Behind him Manning could hear the low murmur of Grimaldi and Roskov as they discussed the mechanics of Barracuda's problem.

The Canadian turned to check the area.

And saw armed, uniformed men breaking out of the trees on the western edge of the clearing. He counted at least six.

Swinging his head around, he saw more coming along the opposite side.

"Damn!" the Phoenix warrior muttered.

Manning got a better look at the advancing troops and something about the way they moved and their formation made him suspect just who they were.

The Phoenix commando reached inside Dragon Slayer and snatched up the handset. He thumbed the transmit button. "Dragon Slayer to Base One," Manning said in a clear, strong voice that revealed little of the tension he felt. "We have unfriendly forces. Appear to be Soviet troops. Probably Spetsnaz commandos. Acknowledge message only, then break contact. Over."

"Acknowledged!" the response came instantly. The voice on the radio sounded more rattled than Manning.

He dropped the handset and grabbed Grimaldi's Uzi from its rack. Grimaldi, closely followed by Roskov, appeared from the brush. Manning tossed the Uzi to the pilot. Grimaldi caught it instinctively and dropped to a kneeling stance, aware Manning must have spotted danger. The Canadian kept low and hurried to their position.

"Those are Kalashnikov rifles, with those curved banana-shaped magazines. Tell me, do Russian navy infantry and airborne units still wear striped T-shirts?" Manning asked Roskov in a whisper as he stared at the commandos, who had moved much closer.

"Yes," the Soviet pilot said with a nod.

"That caps it," Manning commented. "They sent a detachment of Spetsnaz shock troops after us."

"Jesus," Grimaldi rasped. "How'd they get here so soon?"

"You want to ask them?" the Canadian replied dryly.

Another group of men materialized in the rain forest. They moved through the bush with greater ease than the Soviet commandos, as men who lived in an environment are more at home in it than those who have simply trained to work in such conditions. Some wore olive-drab fatigues and jungle camou uniforms. Others were in baggy civilian clothing. Their headgear varied from caps to wide-brimmed straw hats. They carried an assortment of weapons, but the AK-47 assault rifle was the favorite choice among the second team. They approached the Spetsnaz troops, but their dark skin and mestizo features revealed they were not Russians.

"The FAR," Manning whispered. He realized Roskov probably had no idea what he meant. The Canadian whispered an explanation, "Local Communist rebels. Guerrillas working with Spetsnaz."

"And they're all looking for us," Grimaldi said grimly.

A crackle of autofire rang out. Bullets shredded the foliage a few feet from their position. The burst had come from the Guatemalan gunmen, obviously eager to engage. One of the Spetsnaz shouted at the FAR terrorists, probably telling them to hold back, but the initial volley encouraged other guerrillas to open fire.

"I think they found us," Roskov hissed through clenched teeth.

Manning raised the SA80, aimed and fired, sending a short burst into his chosen target. A Guatemalan guerrilla threw his arms wide and flopped back into the ferns and tall grass, two 5.56 mm slugs buried in his chest. The sudden demise of one of their comrades caused the other FAR terrorists to forget their bravura and scramble for cover.

The Canadian tracked a running gunman with the sights of his SA80. He fired again, putting another Marxist conscript face down in the long grass. The man lay kicking and screaming as the capering monkeys in the trees above screeched in mimicry and the sky came alive with startled birds.

A number of weapons opened up, sending a hail of bullets into the dense thicket of trees and foliage.

"These guys mean business," Manning said.

"Yeah, and I don't see an easy way home," Grimaldi pointed out.

He turned abruptly as a lean figure clad in grubby white cotton pants and shirt forced his way through the undergrowth. The Guatemalan guerrilla carried an M-16, which he was firing from the hip. Ignoring the lash of 5.56 mm slugs, Jack Grimaldi tracked the guerrilla with his Uzi, triggering a short burst that slammed the guy in the chest. The impact spun the guerrilla off course and bounced him into the trunk of a tree. The man crashed to the ground in a spray of red.

Manning found himself similarly occupied when a couple more of the overeager Guatemalan Communists came hurtling through the foliage, their auto-weapons raking the way ahead with howling death. Without the foresight of gaining target acquisition, the Guatemalan rebels had relied on firing blind and hoping for a hit through saturation. But they failed to hit any target, and at the same time clearly defined their own presence.

And that was all Gary Manning required. His SA80 ejected a stream of empty shell casings as the Canadian triggered a hail of lead that ended the lives of the reckless pair. Blasted off their feet, the luckless rebels were left writhing their final moments away in spreading pools of their own blood.

During the scant seconds it took for Manning and Grimaldi to take out their opponents, Ilya Roskov found himself face-to-face with his potential executioner. The young Russian had turned to find a swarthy, pockmarked Guatemalan in the act of raising his AK-47. It was clear to Roskov that the rebel intended to fire, and in that moment the asylum-seeking pilot realized that he was very close to becoming extinct. There was no time for any thoughts about what needed doing—Roskov simply reacted as he had been taught to react in a threatening situation. He was barely aware of the Makarov pistol in his hand, or even of leveling it. There was only the sound of a single shot. The bullet chopped a hole between the rebel's eyes, drilling through to his brain. The Guatemalan guerrilla sagged, then slumped to the ground in an ungainly motion, dead before he was horizontal.

"This is getting serious," Grimaldi said with great understatement.

"Let's move," Manning suggested. "Back into the forest. We have to try and lose them."

It was plain from the start that carrying out such a maneuver was not going to work. Despite the indiscipline of the Guatemalan rebels, the superior training of the Spetsnaz began to show. They had not as yet fired a single shot. Instead, the Soviet specialists had spread out, forming a wide semicircle that enabled them to entrap Manning, Grimaldi and Roskov. Now the Spetsnaz troops began to close the semicircle, moving in to surround their quarry. The Soviet commandos used the dense foliage and trees for cover and concealment effectively, yet it was obvious the enemy forces were more numerous than Manning had at first thought. The Spetsnaz and their FAR comrades formed a human net around the area that trapped Manning, Grimaldi and Roskov in the center of an armed ring.

"It's no good," Grimaldi rasped as he tried to aim his Uzi at a shape that ducked behind a tree before he could open fire. "They know the jungle and we don't. Bastards have got us boxed in. All exits closed."

"So we have to make an exit," Manning replied, and tried to determine which direction offered the least resistance.

He glimpsed an object being launched through the air toward their position. A grenade, he realized. The sound of something hitting the bushes less than a hundred yards from them in a different direction announced that the Spetsnaz were using a two-pronged attack and striking simultaneously.

"Down!" the Canadian shouted, and threw himself at Roskov to bring him to the ground.

Roskov grunted under Manning's weight as the Phoenix pro shielded him with his own body. Grimaldi landed on the ground next to them and covered his head with his arms. Manning slung one arm around his own skull and held on to the SA80 with his other hand.

Explosions roared from the jungle. Clumps of earth and uprooted plants showered down on them as a shock wave struck with stunning force. The Spetsnaz had used concussion grenades, purposely tossing them far enough from the trio to daze them with a minimal risk of injury. They wanted Roskov and his companions alive.

Manning rolled off Roskov's prone body. His ears were ringing, and his entire body felt as if it had been slammed with a giant paddle. He could barely make out Grimaldi groaning and cursing under his breath, but his own vision was blurred and he could only hope the pilot wasn't hurt. Roskov stirred next to him, moving slowly like a half-crushed beetle. The Canadian shook his head to clear it. He had worked with explosives all his adult life, and it wasn't the first time he had been so close when a blast occurred. Manning shook off the effects quicker than his companions and glanced up to see several men rushing toward them.

He tried to raise the SA80, but a FAR fanatic closed in rapidly and stamped a boot on the assault rifle, pinning it to the ground. The terrorist raised his own AK-47 and prepared to use it as a club. Powered by fear, anger and sheer determination, Manning thrust himself upward from the ground and drove a fist to his opponent's midsection. The Guatemalan gasped with pain and surprise, then tried to swing the Kalashnikov, but Manning rammed a shoulder into the man and sent him stumbling backward into some of his fellows.

"¡Cabrón!" another terrorist snarled as he tried to attack Manning from behind, prepared to stamp the buttstock of an Uzi subgun into the base of the Phoenix man's neck.

Jack Grimaldi lashed out with both legs and caught the gunman's shins and ankles in a scissors grip. He rolled onto his back, throwing his opponent off balance and sending him tumbling to the ground. Grimaldi started to rise with his own Uzi in his fists, but a well-placed kick sent the subgun hurling from his hands.

"Sneaky bastard," Grimaldi rasped as he quickly grabbed his opponent's ankle. He noticed the boot was black leather without laces, and glanced up just as the Spetsnaz trooper prepared to swing the barrel of a Dragunov rifle. Grimaldi twisted the captive ankle hard and pushed. The Soviet trooper staggered and bobbed around in an effort to keep his footing. Grimaldi lashed out a kick, and drove the toe of his boot into the Spetsnaz's kidney.

The Russian groaned and plunged to the ground as Grimaldi stood up. A FAR terrorist swung a rifle butt at his face, but Grimaldi dodged the swing and kicked him in the gut. As the terrorist doubled up, Grimaldi slammed a fist between his shoulder blades to knock the man to the ground. He was preparing to sideline the Guatemalan for a while when a gun barrel suddenly appeared in front of his face.

"Time out, huh?" Grimaldi said as he gasped for breath and raised his hands in surrender.

The gun muzzle stared back at him. The weapon was in the hands of a Spetsnaz officer who glared at Grimaldi as if he would enjoy squeezing the trigger if he got even the slightest excuse. More Soviet troops and FAR killers swarmed the area. Lieutenant Roskov started to rise from the ground, still dizzy from the concussion blasts. A short-tempered Guatemalan stepped forward and kicked him in the face. The Russian pilot fell on his back, a ribbon of blood at the corner of his mouth.

Gary Manning still fought with three FAR terrorists, too preoccupied to notice how many opponents had arrived on the scene. He hit one Guatemalan Marxist with a solid left, and the man staggered from the blow. A movement warned Manning that another opponent was gearing up to deliver a blow. The Canadian raised his right forearm to block the attack, hitting the second opponent's wrist. He was surprised and alarmed to see a machete pop out of the guy's hand. He hadn't noticed the big jungle knife before he saw the swing coming, and the Canadian was astonished his arm wasn't chopped off at the elbow.

An elbow, indeed, flashed through his mind as he smashed the point of his elbow into his opponent's face. The FAR flunky tumbled to the ground in a dazed heap as another terrorist stepped forward and swung a right cross to Manning's jaw. The Canadian's head rocked from the punch, but he responded with a kick to the attacker's groin. The guerrilla doubled over with a wail of agony, and Manning slammed him under the jaw with an upper cut that lifted the guy off his feet and dropped him senseless into the arms of one of his comrades.

Manning whirled around and started to reach for his Walther P-5 in shoulder leather. He froze in midaction as he saw half a dozen weapons pointed in his direction and other guns aimed at Grimaldi and Roskov. Reluctantly the Canadian raised his empty hands to shoulder level.

"Is it too late for diplomacy?" Manning asked, trying to sound less concerned than he felt.

A big Spetsnaz glowered at him from under his black beret, then moved in and rammed the muzzle of his rifle into Manning's stomach. The Canadian doubled over and moaned from the sharp pain in his belly. The Russian soldier reached out and plucked the Walther from shoulder leather.

"That's what I thought," Manning muttered through clenched teeth.

3

"This is urgent," Hal Brognola announced as he sat at the head of the conference table at the Stony Man War Room. "It concerns Gary."

The four members of Phoenix Force at the table were instantly attentive and sat up tensely in their chairs. They were accustomed to receiving extremely important information about missions to hot spots throughout the world—missions that often concerned the fate of nations and world peace. Although they were used to dealing with assignments that involved the defense of the United States and the free world, it was not the same as hearing that one of their own was in danger.

"What about Gary?" Rafael Encizo inquired. The Cuban's handsome dark features were clouded by concern, and an edge of urgency affected his voice.

Brognola explained what had happened to Gary Manning and Jack Grimaldi, from their training tests with Dragon Slayer to their journey to the Guatemalan jungle to rescue Ilya Roskov and retrieve Barracuda.

"Why in the bloody hell was Gary with Jack in the Dragon Slayer?" David McCarter demanded. The tall Briton had left his seat to begin pacing like a caged lion. "I'm the chopper pilot. Hell, if it's got wings or rotor blades, I can fly it...."

"Please, David," Yakov Katzenelenbogen, the unit commander of Phoenix Force said softly. "Go on, Hal."

"The last word I got on Gary and Jack came via the USS *Anaconda*," Brognola continued. "Gary radioed from the jungle to state that Soviet Spetsnaz troops had arrived. Then he broke contact and told *Anaconda* to do likewise."

"That way the radio transmission from the aircraft carrier wouldn't be directly linked with Dragon Slayer if the chopper fell into enemy hands," Katz remarked as he placed his right elbow on the table. A prosthesis was attached to the stump of this arm, which ended at the elbow. He placed his left hand over the curved portion of the steel hooks at the end of the artificial limb as he added, "Gary followed proper security procedure. If he goes down, he doesn't want the U.S. Navy involved in an unsanctioned action on Guatemalan soil."

"Yeah," Calvin James replied, and a slight smile tugged at the lanky black commando's lips. "Gary would think about saving the other guy's ass when his own was in the fire. Where the hell did the Spetsnaz troops come from? Did that Soviet carrier manage to send them that fast? How did they manage to catch up with our guys and this Russian defector without having the exact coordinates? Dragon Slayer would have had a helluva time finding the downed MiG in the jungle without them. Figure those Russian experiments on ESP finally paid off?"

"Does it matter?" McCarter demanded. "Gary said they were Spetsnaz, and that makes it true. How they got there and what they're doing in Guatemala hardly matters. What *does* matter is that we've got to go in and get our mates out of there."

"I know," the Fed stated, "but this is a delicate situation. We have Gary and Jack in Guatemala without any kind of sanction. The President didn't okay this action, so my ass could be in a sling, too. That's not a big deal unless it jeopardizes Stony Man operations in the future. Gary and Jack are facing things that are a lot worse. Even if the Russians didn't get them, the place is crawling with FAR terrorists."

"Fuerzas Armadas Revolucionario," Encizo said with a nod. "I was in Mexico in the late 1970s when there was a lot of concern about the 23rd September Communist League that was involved in many incidents of violent sabotage and murders at the time. One of the biggest worries was that the 23rd SCL might link up with their comrades in the FAR across the border in Guatemala. The FAR has a reputation for extreme brutality and ruthlessness—even by terrorist standards. Of course, Guatemala itself doesn't have the greatest reputation when it comes to human rights."

"That's another problem we've got," Brognola said with a grim nod. "The United States government cut off aid to Guatemala about ten years ago because the country had such a bad record on human rights. Amnesty International claims there were at least five thousand political murders carried out by death squads. Guatemala's government was still rotten with corruption back in 1982... and probably continued after that. They had one military coup after another until they finally had honest-to-God elections in 1986 and got the first civilian president in decades. A lot of people question how fair those elections were, though, and just what kind of government is really running the country these days."

"So if the local military forces find Gary and Jack, they could wind up in prison," James said grimly. "Or shot as spies or some such bullshit."

"True," Katz remarked with a sigh. The middle-aged Israeli looked at his teammates and added, "That's a risk we'll all be taking when we go in after them."

"So, what are we waiting for?" McCarter demanded eagerly.

"Let's think for a minute," the Phoenix commander urged. "It's highly possible the Spetsnaz captured our friends and Roskov. The question is, what would they do with them? The Soviets aren't sanctioned in Guatemala, either. It's hard to imagine they got the Spetsnaz inland from the Soviet carrier so quickly. That suggests the Spetsnaz were already there, probably working with the FAR terrorist cells as advisers, just as they were doing in Nicaragua with the special forces training camps the Soviets set up after Ortega took control."

"But Spetsnaz operations in Nicaragua were authorized by Moscow and Managua," Encizo reminded him. "Guatemala City wouldn't agree to having the Spetsnaz in the country, and Moscow is trying to promote a new image worldwide with this *glasnost* business."

"It's possible the Soviet government isn't even aware of such activity in Guatemala," Katz stated. "Technically Spetsnaz shock troops work under the direction of the GRU military Intelligence. However, GRU wouldn't be bucking the Secretary General's wishes unless they could count on enormous support from the Soviet military. Since they can't, that suggests somebody else is responsible for the Spetsnaz operations in Guatemala."

"Who else?" McCarter replied with a snort. "It has to be the KGB."

"We do know Gorbachev's reforms are not going down well with some of the Politburo members," Brognola added. "That would go double for some of the high-muckety-mucks in the KGB. The Secretary General replaced the old boss of the Committee for State Security, but there are still enough of the old guard in the KGB who would see the new policies as a total sellout. For that matter, some in the new guard might not like seeing the KGB lose a lot of its power, either."

"Well, if the KGB is behind the Spetsnaz in Guatemala," Katz continued, "I don't think they'll be inclined to kill Gary, Jack or Roskov if they can help it. They'll want to obtain information first, and possibly use them to try for a deal with the U.S. government. Exchange them for Soviet agents held in the United States or, more likely, attempt to pressure Uncle Sam into using its influence. It would make FAR happy if the Guatemalan government released some political prisoners."

"Yeah," James said as he looked down at the table. "Or it could be the Russians shot 'em down as soon as they caught up with them in the jungle."

"I'm not going to believe they're dead until I see it with my own eyes," McCarter insisted.

"Hal, we know the risks," Katz assured the Stony Man boss. "Get us into Guatemala. I don't care how. We'll take it from there."

"I can get you in," Brognola assured him. "The tough part will be after you're in the country and pretty much on your own."

"Pretty much?" Encizo asked with raised eyebrows. "Is that a glimmer of hope that you can get us some sort of contact in Guatemala?"

"Hey, I'm not just a pretty face," Brognola declared as he peeled off the cellophane wrapper from a cigar and stuck it in his mouth. "I've had Aaron working on the computers to come up with a lead for us. We used one of our front outfits to get some cooperation from the CIA control officer in Mexico City, who in turn contacted the CIA case officer in Guatemala City. He's stationed at the U.S. Embassy there. Isn't that original?"

"That's what you can expect from the Company," Encizo said dryly. He was a veteran of the Bay of Pigs invasion and didn't have a high opinion of the CIA.

"Well, he has a couple of guys in the field in Guatemala," the Fed continued. "The one we got is the son of a Guatemalan immigrant, born in the U.S. He speaks Spanish with a Guatemalan accent. His name is José Rios Castillo."

"I hope he's no stranger to the jungle," James commented. "Most of the Intelligence people we've worked with over the years are city boys. They'd be lucky not to get lost in a public park in broad daylight.''

''That's why we got Rios,'' Brognola answered. ''He's been operating out of the rain forests in Guatemala for some time. Radio listening posts, Intelligence gathering about rebel groups such as Contras based in El Salvador, as well as leftist outfits like the FAR and the ERP. CIA tries to keep tabs on the guys who are supposedly working on our side as well as those working for the opposition.''

''Good enough,'' Katz stated. ''How soon can you get us out of here and on our way to Guatemala?''

''You guys go pack your gear,'' Brognola replied. ''By the time you're ready to leave, your plane will be revving up for takeoff.''

4

Salazar wanted to kill the captives immediately. Angry at the loss of a number of his men, the Guatemalan Communist rebel leader was in a vengeful mood. He wanted blood for blood.

"I want their heads!" he raged wildly. "Those Yankee *bastards* have killed many of my best men."

Captain Viktor Kirov, the commander of the Spetsnaz squad, listened in weary silence to the ranting of the dark-haired, stocky Guatemalan. He and his men had been training the local subversives for the past two weeks, and the Russian's patience was wearing thin. Salazar was a Cuban-indoctrinated Marxist, his mind full of worn clichés about American imperialism, Yankee capitalists and any number of similar phrases most probably written by Castro himself. If Kirov had not been a professional military man, he would have probably eliminated the tiresome little man after the first few days. But that wasn't allowed to happen. Kirov and his men had been sent to Guatemala on a covert mission. Their task was to train and equip Salazar and his band of rebels. The objective was the destruction of one of the country's most valuable oil fields.

Guatemala did not have much of an economy. Its oil production was one of its most valuable assets. Most of its oil was exported to the United States, and though the destruction of the production facility—cutting off the flow of oil to America—would not hurt the U.S. too much, it would damage the Guatemalan economy. Rocking the country's already shaky economy would create unrest. Destabilizing the population made it easier for the rebel groups to increase their propaganda drive.

The KGB, in its infinite wisdom, had selected Kirov and his squad for the mission. Kirov had a sound record. He had conducted a number of successful missions in Afghanistan and Africa and was known for his dedication and resourcefulness. His name had been at the head of the list the moment the Guatemalan mission came up.

The unexpected call from the *Pushkin*, with fresh orders, had done little to confuse Kirov. He had undertaken the task of seeking out the downed Barracuda and its pilot without question. He hadn't expected to be confronted by American specialists sent in to meet Roskov, but again that was part of a soldier's lot. If you didn't adapt, you failed, and at worst you died. The only complication had been Salazar and his trigger-happy rebels.

"There will be no killing of prisoners unless I order it," Kirov stated flatly. "Roskov is to be returned to the Soviet Union, so he must be kept alive. The Americans are too valuable to be destroyed on a personal whim. You must learn to control your emotions, Salazar. Rise above petty motives of revenge."

"What of my men?" the guerrilla leader demanded. "They are dead because of these Yankee dogs."

Kirov sighed. "Your men are dead because they lacked the discipline of true professionals and went up against superior fighters. Face it, Salazar, your men were totally outclassed."

Anger raged in Salazar's eyes. He held Kirov's steady gaze, well aware that the Russian was laughing at him behind the impassive expression on his face. What made matters worse was the fact that Kirov's words held a great deal of truth. The Americans were good fighters, however much he hated to admit it.

"So, what do we do now?" the Guatemalan asked.

"Leave some men to guard the plane and helicopter," Kirov said. "The rest of us return to base and await the arrival of the retrieval squad."

"What about our mission?" Salazar wanted to know.

"The oil field won't go away. A delay of a few more days won't cause any problems. It will give your men more time to practice. Some of them could use it."

"Tell me something, Captain Kirov," Salazar said. "Why do you dislike me so much?"

"Does it show?" Kirov smiled. "I do not like your brand of politics, Salazar. You are a little man with restricted vision. World revolution on a grand scale is too vast for you to comprehend. All you see is this stinking patch of jungle and a picture of yourself riding into Guatemala City in the back of a jeep as the nation's liberator. And then what, Salazar? Another Cuba? Another anachronistic Communist state where everything stays the same? No ambition, no advancement, just marking time until the people become disenchanted because the new regime has given little better than the old one."

"It is our duty to liberate our brothers from the capitalist yoke," Salazar answered. "We must rid ourselves of the influence of the Americans and their exploitation of the poor."

"I see," Kirov said. "That's what it's all about, is it? The almighty Yankee dollar."

Salazar stared at the Spetsnaz officer as if he was seeing a stranger. "I do not understand you," he said slowly. "Don't you want to destroy the Americans?"

"We are in a war of ideologies now, Salazar. The old days of painting Americans as slavering, money-hungry murderers are past. They are still our enemy—there is no denying that. But matters have taken on a different form. The struggle is on a much more subtle level now. Subversion and terrorism still have their place and always will. But overall, the long-term plan has become low-profile. It works at a slower pace, still with the same objective, but it has become accepted that major changes in the world power bases will only be achieved through determined persistence. By breaking away the foundations of democracy, bit by little bit. Not by ranting and raving and screaming about the stereotype Americans who are responsible for every atrocity the world has seen. Only those who refuse to see any other image really believe such nonsense."

Salazar shook his head. "I am not sure I understand what you are talking about. My concern is for my people and the struggle we have with the government. There is only one way we will get rid of them, and that is by destroying everything they consider important."

"Let us return to base," Kirov said. "We can discuss this matter further."

The Russian only wanted an excuse to end the conversation. He was aware of Salazar's limited outlook, and the man had gone out of his way to prove his ignorance simply by opening his mouth.

Without another word the Spetsnaz commander strode across to where his men were standing guard around the three captives.

"Well, gentlemen," he said in good English, "you may be pleased to know that we are leaving now. There is a long walk ahead of you and nowhere to run, should you decide to try to escape."

"What do you have in store for us at the end of this little stroll?" Manning asked.

Kirov smiled. "That is as unknown to me as it must be to you," he explained. "Your fate is still hanging in the balance at this moment. That is, until I receive my orders concerning your future."

"Great news," Grimaldi muttered as Kirov moved on to relay commands to his Spetsnaz troops.

Kirov shouted something in Russian. Four Spetsnaz commandos, along with six guerrillas, broke away from the main group and watched as Kirov led the rest away. Manning, Grimaldi and Roskov were pushed roughly into motion, surrounded by the unsmiling Spetsnaz troops.

They marched across the clearing and into the maw of the noisy, living jungle.

For the next three hours they trudged through the tangle of trees and vines, which was intertwined with large ferns and the tall grass that grew in abundance due to the moist, steamy atmosphere. The lushness of the forest was much in evidence. The greenery had a vibrant, living color, and gave way in spots to the heavy, overripe fruits and bright splashes of tropical flowers.

Everywhere the jungle teemed with noisy life. This was no silent forest. Bird song erupted constantly, frequently more a raucous shriek or a shrill whistling. The flitting shapes of capering monkeys in the high branches were accompanied by unbroken chatter, and at ground level lesser creatures added their croaks and chirrups or the slithering sounds of movement.

As they moved deeper into the forest, the bright sunlight of the day was lost. The canopy formed by the uppermost branches cut off a greater part of the natural light, leaving the lower levels in a perpetual gloom. Here and there great shafts of sunlight lanced down through the branches, burying their ends in the earth. Dust motes swam lazily in the beams of light, graceful in their silence.

The lofty roof of intermingled leaves trapped heat and moisture. The ground underfoot was damp and spongy, the air thick and cloyingly scented by the perfume of exotic flowers that somehow managed an unlikely blend with the underlying scent of decay.

Within a half hour of commencing the march, every man was dripping with sweat. Clothing clung damply to wet flesh. The pores simply opened and exuded moisture. The sweat irritated the skin, stung the eyes and trickled into mouths, leaving a salty tang on the lips.

More than once they had to wade through pools of brackish, scummy water. The water was warm, and below the surface wriggling creatures swam away from the moving objects. Beneath the feet of the wading men, soft mud was disturbed, sometimes releasing large bubbles of trapped air that would rise speedily to the surface to burst and release stale air and gas.

As they moved deeper inland, the forest became even denser, and the tangled undergrowth seemed to close in around them. Toward the end of the third hour they started to ascend, following a barely visible trail that worked its way up the side of a towering escarpment of rock and vegetation. The climb was slow because the way was thick with entwined vines and clumps of high ferns. It was difficult to see where the solid ground lay beneath the rich grass or where the edge of the trail fell into space. Below them the canopy of the forest looked like a solid green carpet.

The long, awkward climb took its toll. Every man in the party moved slowly, aware of the ever-present heat and the way it could sap their strength. Tempers were beginning to fray at the edges. It was preordained that at some point someone would reach his limit.

When it happened it came so fast no one had any time to react. One moment they were all moving doggedly up the faint trail, the next a wild outburst shattered the afternoon calm.

One of Salazar's guerrillas, who had been allowing his frustration and anger to grow, lost control when Jack Grimaldi stumbled awkwardly. The Guatemalan, bitter at the loss of a number of his comrades at the hands of the Americans used Grimaldi's hesitation to vent his rage. Yelling incoherently in Spanish, he drove the butt of his AK-47 into the small of Grimaldi's back, drawing a shout of pain and anger from the flyer.

"You dirty bastard!" Grimaldi yelled back. He twisted around and, despite the fact that he was facing an armed man, lashed out with his booted foot, landing a numbing blow to the thigh. "Touch me again and I'll make you eat that friggin' Commie BB gun."

The Guatemalan did not understand English, but he recognized the venom in Grimaldi's retort and allowed it to fuel his own wild, unreasoning anger. Spitting foul obscenities, he swung his weapon at Grimaldi a second time. He put all his strength into the intended blow, aiming for Grimaldi's head.

Grimaldi saw the blow coming and ducked out of the way. The AK-47 missed, and the force of the swing pulled the Guatemalan almost on top of the Stony Man pilot. Grimaldi was so tired and hot and sweaty, as well as good and mad, that he lost his head for a few seconds. He slammed his right knee into the rebel's groin, ripping a startled screech from the guy's throat. The guerrilla swung his right hand in a cracking blow that rattled Grimaldi's teeth as it caught his lower jaw.

Neither man realized how close they had slithered to the edge of the trail during their brief but heated conflict. It only became noticeable when the Guatemalan lost his balance. His eyes bulged in terror as he began his fall, and in pure panic and reflex he reached out to grab something. That something turned out to be Jack Grimaldi's shirt. It was all it took to drag Grimaldi beyond the point of no return.

Split seconds later Grimaldi and the Guatemalan had lurched off the edge of the trail and were cartwheeling down the steep slope, crashing through tangled undergrowth and ferns. A shower of loosened earth and stones trailed in their wake.

"Jack!" Gary Manning yelled, forgetting cover names and everything else as he watched in horror.

The tumbling, twisting bodies slithered over an outcropping some fifty feet down the slope, then dropped through empty space before crashing through the canopy of treetops farther below. The sound of cracking branches and rustling leaves floated back up to the silent line of men who had witnessed the fall.

Kirov broke the trance.

"We have wasted enough time," he snapped in curt Spanish. "Come, we have far to go yet."

Gary Manning was less than fluent in Spanish, but he understand enough of Kirov's orders to realize the Soviet officer intended to abandon both Grimaldi and the guerrilla to whatever fate had in store for them at the bottom of the ravine.

"What about my partner?" Manning demanded in English from Kirov. "We can't just leave him. He may be badly hurt."

"True. He may also be dead," the Russian said with a shrug. "Either way, he is of no further use or interest to me."

"You son of a bitch..." Manning began, but realized angry insults would not make Kirov more agreeable. "Look, Captain. You want to question us and get information from us. Right? A dead man can't tell you anything. We could go down and search for him...."

"How do you propose we reach him?" Kirov asked. "The only way would be to return to the base of the slope, then work our way around the area and penetrate the forest to bring us directly below where we are now. That could take us a day. Maybe longer. I don't have the time. Nor the interest."

Manning fell silent, aware that he wasn't going to get anywhere talking to Kirov. The Spetsnaz commander had no feelings concerning Grimaldi's or the FAR guerrilla's welfare. If Kirov didn't give a damn about a Marxist "comrade" on his side, he certainly couldn't be moved to care about a "capitalist imperialist" enemy. Manning realized that if Grimaldi was alive down there, he was going to have to fend for himself. On a different level Manning was going to have to do the same. It was a time of pure survival for both of them. They could expect no help or assistance from anyone. It was all going to have to come through their own efforts.

The Canadian recognized he was still treating Grimaldi as a functioning unit. He had no real knowledge of the flyer's condition, but until he had it confirmed, he would not allow himself to accept that Grimaldi might be dead. That was negative thinking. As far as he was concerned, Grimaldi was still alive. Hurt maybe, but alive, and Grimaldi would fight to stay that way. The pilot was a tough nut. If he still had breath in him, he would drag himself out of the jungle.

Raised voices caught Manning's attention. Kirov and Salazar were having another heated discussion, no doubt concerning the fate of Salazar's man. Kirov indeed wasn't much concerned about the guerrilla. If the man still lived, he wasn't worth the cost of a long, tiring trek back through the forest. Salazar plainly didn't see the argument, but he knew his priorities. He also knew the power Kirov wielded, and wasn't about to buck the Soviet's decision. After much grumbling the Guatemalan rebel did as he was told and returned to his men.

"We go," Kirov said, and the march continued.

5

It took a while for the fact to sink in, but finally Jack Grimaldi accepted that he was still alive. Not exactly kicking, but very much in the land of the living. After all, only living things hurt.

It was dark, and the trauma had left him feeling stiff and cold.

And there was pain. His entire body throbbed, each fiber of his being aching fiercely.

Consciousness was returning in a series of overlapping waves. Awake, then drifting back, then awake again. Each time he woke it was for a longer period than the last, until he finally lay completely alert, staring up at small patches of the night sky visible through the canopy of trees.

He knew he would have to move soon. He needed to find cover for the night.

Before that he had to establish the extent of his injuries.

Arms and legs first. Gentle movements, flexing fingers and toes. Stiffness, but no sharp pain to indicate broken bones. That was something to be grateful for. He found he could also move his head. Raising his hands, he moved them over his upper body, probing gently. When he touched his ribs down the left side, pain exploded with a vengeance. Grimaldi felt sweat break through his skin. He groaned, not caring whether anyone heard, though he doubted there would be anyone there. After a time he explored the area again. It was sore. Really sore, but he felt certain there was no fracture. Severe bruising was his diagnosis, but he was also well aware that he might easily be mistaken.

The next task was sitting up. He took it very cautiously, a couple of inches at a time, until he was upright. He was panting by the time he achieved it, and his body was protesting like crazy. The effort left him sick and giddy, and he sat motionless for some time before trying to move again. Next he tried climbing to his feet, and the effort almost made him pass out. He had to turn onto his hands and knees, then work his way upright in a series of spasmodic movements that reduced him to quivering, sweaty jelly. When he was eventually upright, he was convinced that he would never walk away from the spot he was on. If he took a single step, he would fall flat on his face and that would be the end.

He decided it was about time to get angry with himself. He used a lot of bad language, doing his best to shame himself out of the mood of helplessness that was threatening to engulf him. It did the trick. He walked. Stiffly, hurting with every step, but he walked.

The problem was, where the hell did he walk to?

He was without direction in the jungle, without weapons or food. Unsure of his exact location, and certainly without friends.

That line of thought made him think about Gary Manning and Ilya Roskov.

Where were they and in what condition? Kirov, the Spetsnaz commander, had made it clear that the lives of his captives were by no means secure. It was obvious from the lack of interest in his own predicament that Kirov did not value Grimaldi's existence too highly. But Grimaldi didn't give a damn how the Russian viewed him. He was just thankful that Kirov's indifference had given him some breathing space.

Nor was Grimaldi slow to realize how lucky he had been to survive his fall. Though darkness prevented him from seeing from what height he'd tumbled down, the flyer knew it had been a considerable distance. He couldn't be certain what had contributed to his survival, but he was sure that the dense canopy of trees had been an important cushioning factor.

Grimaldi wondered how the Guatemalan guerrilla had fared. Had he survived, and if so, where was he? The possibility that he was also alive added another dangerous element to Grimaldi's situation. The Stony Man flyer realized he was going to need to keep his presence under wraps, and he called himself every kind of a fool for his earlier outburst.

Grimaldi faded into the deeper shadows at the foot of the escarpment. He found what he was looking for after twenty minutes of searching.

A shallow depression close to the ground with a jutting overhang of rock forming a crude roof. Grimaldi collected an armful of long ferns. He used some to cover the ground beneath the overhang. The rest he used to conceal the depression after he had stretched himself out. There was little else he could do under the circumstances. It was pointless blundering around in the near darkness. Grimaldi decided to rest until first light, then make his plans.

6

The Boeing CH-46 Sea Knight helicopter hovered six feet above the pale strip of beach, its rotor wash frothing the water that lapped at the sand. At a signal from the Marine sergeant framed in the open doorway, four figures clad in jungle camou fatigues and laden with equipment exited the helicopter.

"Good luck, guys," the Marine said.

Moments later the Boeing turned about and swept away from the beach, vanishing into the night. The beat of its motor faded quickly.

A marked silence replaced the chopper's noise. The silence held until one of the men from the Boeing made a characteristic comment.

"How come we never get any bleeding girls in grass skirts coming out to welcome us?"

"Wrong part of the Pacific, pal," Calvin James explained.

"Story of my bloody life," McCarter said. "Always in the wrong place at the wrong time."

"I hope that doesn't apply when we find ourselves in a combat situation," Encizo said.

McCarter's white teeth flashed in the gloom. "I make exceptions then."

"Okay," Katz butted in. "Clowning time is now over. That's official. Let's go and see if we can tie up with our contact man."

Phoenix Force had hit the Guatemalan beachhead.

Hal Brognola had worked wonders in his efforts to get Phoenix Force en route to Guatemala. Within two hours of the briefing the Stony Man team was on board a government Lear jet streaking skyward from Bolling Air Force Base. The Lear cut a direct route across the country, landing briefly at Randolph AFB in Texas for refueling. Airborne once more, it left the Lone Star State far behind as it headed out over the Gulf of Mexico. At a high altitude it flew over Yucatan and then Quintana Roo before descending in a wide curve that brought it on the final leg of its flight. The blue water of the Caribbean Sea flashed beneath as the Lear made its approach to the international airport at Stanley Field, not far from Belize City in the nation of Belize—formerly known as British Honduras.

High-level discussions had been underway between Washington and the British government in London. With the cooperation of the British and the British military authorities in Belize, permission was granted for the Lear to land at Stanley Field. Even while the Lear was on its way, four U.S. Navy Harrier V/ STOLs—Vertical and Short Take Off and Landing— fighter jets blasted off from the USS *Anaconda*. They flew at high altitude across Guatemala and landed in a remote corner of the Stanley Field airport. They sat beneath the hot sun and waited for the arrival of the Lear and its mysterious passengers.

The Lear touched down at dusk, taxiing across the runway to park beside the four Navy jets. After brief formalities had been exchanged, Phoenix Force divided up their gear and each climbed into the spare seat of a Harrier. The V/STOLs powered up and rose effortlessly into the Belize sunset. Minutes later they were hurtling into the darkening sky, gaining altitude before making the return journey across Belize and Guatemala.

With touchdown on the *Anaconda*'s flight deck, Phoenix Force was escorted directly into a meeting with Captain Garner, the carrier's commander. Garner had already been instructed to cooperate with the visitors in every way possible. They explained that they would need to be transported by Navy helicopter to a prearranged spot and be dropped at a beach. They did not tell him that they planned to rendezvous with CIA agent Rios after they arrived in Guatemala.

Hot food and coffee was provided for the Phoenix team as they prepared for the mission. Once they were in their camou fatigues, the Stony Man warriors inspected their weapons and made sure they had ample ammunition.

Between gulps of hot coffee, Calvin James checked his M-16 assault rifle and fixed the M-203 grenade launcher to the underside of the barrel. The black warrior carried spare magazines of 5.56 mm ammunition for the weapon, as well as a selection of explosive 40 mm rounds for the launcher. His Beretta 92-F double action 9 mm pistol went into his shoulder holster rig, and his G-96 Jet Aer knife was sheathed on his belt. Along with the arms, James also carried a medical pack, since one of his functions was as team medic.

Happy because the U.S. Navy had provided him with as much iced Coke as he could drink, David McCarter loaded his Intertec KG-99 SMG with a 36-round magazine of 9 mm bullets. He was already sporting his 9 mm Browning Hi-Power and the fearsome Gerber Predator combat knife he favored. He clipped a number of fragmentation grenades to his combat harness, adding a few concussion grenades, as well.

Heckler and Koch provided both handgun and SMG for Rafael Encizo. The Cuban had used his MP-5 subgun for a long time. He was also satisfied with the P-95 autopistol he now carried. Both weapons took 9 mm. Encizo's knife, as always, was the Cold Steel Tanto.

Laying aside his loaded Uzi, Katz quickly checked his SIG-Sauer P226 autopistol. Slipping the handgun into its holster, the Israeli lit a last cigarette and sat back for a few quiet moments. He knew that once the mission got under way, there would be little opportunity for relaxing. The missions the Force undertook were alike in one respect. They were never dull and were, for the most part, dangerous and full of surprises.

A knock on the door preceded the entry of a young Marine officer. "We're ready when you are," he said.

Katz stubbed out his cigarette and stood up. Slinging his pack over one shoulder, he picked up his Uzi. "Gentlemen, shall we go?"

Now the USS *Anaconda* was far out to sea, and Phoenix Force was alone on a Guatemalan beach.

Katz pulled a map from his pocket and shook it open. As he did that, Encizo produced a small flashlight, playing the beam of light on the map.

"Rios will be waiting in a panel truck on this dirt road," the Israeli explained, indicating a marked point on the chart. "It should take about an hour to an hour and a half to reach it."

"Providing we don't run into any army patrols along the way," James observed.

"According to intelligence reports, the Guatemalan army is stretched pretty thin," Katz said. "This particular area has been quiet for about six months, so little military presence has been needed."

"Either Guatemalan Intelligence isn't as sharp as it should be," James said, "or somebody is suppressing information."

"It could be true that no one has seen anything," McCarter pointed out. "This is remote country. Jungle like this can hide a lot of activity."

"Whatever the reason," Katz said, "we've got to work within the limits of our information."

Replacing the map, Katz motioned to the group to move out. He took the lead himself, with McCarter on his heels. Next came Calvin James. At the rear Encizo monitored the trail behind them.

The Force moved steadily inland, pushing through dense forest that was alive with the sounds of the night creatures. As well as the unseen noisemakers, they had to contend with the insects that were attracted by the warm, living flesh of the Phoenix warriors.

It took them slightly over two hours to reach the road.

The narrow, rutted track that passed for a road appeared before them, a pale strip under the early morning's thin, gray light. Katz raised a warning hand, then signaled for everyone to get down.

Long minutes passed. Nothing stirred on the road. No travelers or traffic. Despite the apparently deserted road, Katz was reluctant to move until he was satisfied.

The map was checked again, and their position pinpointed as close as possible with the compass.

"By these coordinates," the Israeli said, "we should be within two miles of the rendezvous point. From here we follow the road north."

At his command the Force moved on, in single file along the edge of the track. They all carried their autoweapons at the ready.

The four commandos were fully alert, aware that their mission, beyond the usual dangers, could very well evolve into something with even greater proportions.

At that precise moment no one had any word as to the fate of Gary Manning or Jack Grimaldi or Ilya Roskov. The three might be captives of the Spetsnaz.

They might also be injured or, at worst, they could even be dead.

But until they gained definite information, the Force considered the three to be alive—and therefore able to be rescued. And for all of them, that meant total commitment to the mission, regardless of the odds.

Katz, still in the lead, held up a warning hand. Everyone stopped and settled into a crouch and waited.

Katz moved forward a few yards, peering into the graying light of the early dawn. Then he about-faced and came back, gathering the Force around him.

"I spotted the van up ahead," he whispered.

"Good," McCarter grumbled. "I'm getting ready for a ride."

"Before you get too excited," Katz warned, "you had better consider this—there are two armed men waiting beside the van."

"Hey, Rios was supposed to be on his own," Encizo said.

"Exactly," Katz replied. "He was also supposed to be sitting inside the van with no lights showing. Now we have two armed men outside the van, and the rear lights are on."

"I begin to smell a setup," Calvin James remarked.

McCarter was the one to voice the thought that had passed through everyone's minds. "You don't think Rios has sold us out, do you?"

"If he had," Katz said, "and was using the van to bait a trap, you wouldn't expect him to change prearranged conditions, would you?"

"That would be crazy," James interjected.

"It would simply make the other party suspicious," Encizo remarked.

"Exactly," the Phoenix commander agreed.

A low chuckle came from McCarter. The Brit's own inbuilt cunning had enabled him to grasp immediately what Katz was suggesting. "I'd say Rios has been hijacked himself. The ones who tagged him have stepped into his place, not realizing Rios has set them up by giving incorrect identification procedures."

"And it's worked," Encizo concluded.

"But knowing all this still leaves a couple of unanswered questions for me," James said. "Are there just the two standing by the van, or is there a whole bunch waiting inside? And are there any others concealed in the undergrowth around the van?"

"We'll have to do a sweep."

"All right," Katz said. "Rafael, you come with me. We'll take this side of the road. David, you and Cal take the other side. We will meet up at the far side of the panel truck."

7

The daylight was penetrating the jungle more swiftly by the minute, threatening to reduce Phoenix Force's cover. The warriors were forced to move with extra caution, aware that the dissipating shadows would no longer hide their passing.

Time had passed too quickly, yet they had to resist the urge to increase their pace. A false move, the slightest noise, could easily alert a well-concealed enemy to their presence. But the members of the elite commando squad were too experienced to jump the gun. They were old hands at this type of procedure.

Katz and Encizo completed their circuit of the parked panel truck and settled back to await the arrival of their partners.

They had seen no sign of hidden forces either close to the truck or in the surrounding jungle area. Both men were satisfied that the full complement of the opposition was by the vehicle itself and maybe inside.

Less than five minutes later McCarter and James eased into view, having barely disturbed a leaf during their approach.

"Nothing," James reported.

"Same here," Encizo confirmed.

"Then it's down to the jokers by the truck," McCarter stated. "And any buddies they might have inside."

"Then let's do it," Katz said. "David, you and Cal take the two beside the truck. Encizo and I will cover the inside. Rafael, you take the rear doors. I'll take the driver's door. Remember, we must keep Rios in mind. He may be alive and inside the truck. If there's any shooting, let's not forget he's on our side."

"How long do you need to get in position?" McCarter asked.

"Five minutes," Katz said. He glanced at Encizo. "That okay for you, Rafael?"

The Cuban nodded, then they all synchronized watches. The four parted without another word. McCarter and James moved so as to be on the far side of the panel truck. From where they were crouching, they had a clear view of the two waiting gunmen.

Thin tendrils of early-morning mist drifted through the undergrowth as the day's heat began to build, drawing moisture from the spongy earth of the jungle floor.

McCarter nudged James. "I don't fancy yours," he whispered, glancing in the direction of the waiting gunmen.

James took a long look at the pair. He nodded in understanding.

"Don't tell me," he said. "Mine's the big ugly one in the T-shirt?"

"You're getting better at this game all the time," McCarter said with an infectious grin.

"No shit," James responded. "What the hell would we do for amusement if you hadn't you came along?"

McCarter's reply was to tap the face of his watch. The waiting time was up.

They slid from the undergrowth without a sound, treading the earth on light feet, swiftly covering the distance between themselves and the waiting sentries.

McCarter had slung his KG-99 from one shoulder by its strap. He had his Browning in his right fist.

He was two steps from his man when there was a yell followed by a loud thump inside the panel truck. A fraction of a second later the crackle of an SMG removed the need for further caution.

McCarter lunged forward, jamming the muzzle of his Hi-Power behind the right ear of his target. The man, a broad-shouldered Guatemalan, stiffened. McCarter slammed his free hand between the man's shoulders, pushing him in toward the side of the truck.

"You stand still, friend, or I'll blow your head wide open," the ex-SAS man warned in his limited Spanish. "And get rid of the gun. Now!"

Calvin James had gone for his man in the same breath, jabbing the muzzle of the M-16 into the small of the back.

Instead of submitting, the big man twisted around. He moved with surprising speed for someone of his bulk. He was at least six foot two, and almost as wide. His left hand, which resembled a catcher's mitt, slapped aside the M-16. The big guy followed through with a driving snap-kick that was aimed for James's groin. At the same time, he made an attempt to level the Uzi he was holding.

James reacted with equal speed, pulling his lean body out of range of the big guy's slashing foot. He allowed himself to fall to the earth, dropping below the Uzi's muzzle. In the instant he touched the ground, the Israeli subgun blasted out a volley of 9 mm slugs, spitting smoking shell casings from its port. The slugs howled over James's head. With the muzzle tilted upward at the big guy, the black warrior's M-16 erupted, sending a trio of 5.56 mm projectiles up into his chest. The force of the bullets knocked the guy back a couple of steps, but he refused to go down and made another attempt at putting his Uzi on target. James shot him again, loosing two bursts this time. Six 5.56 mm slugs hammered the big man's chest. He exhaled with a deep grunt, swaying, the muzzle of the Uzi suddenly pointing at the sky. His finger pulled down on the trigger, emptying the magazine at the treetops. Then he toppled sideways, hitting the ground with a solid thud.

Rafael Encizo's left hand had barely touched the handle of the rear door of the panel truck when someone gave a loud yell from inside the vehicle. There was a crash as the doors were kicked open, and a man carrying an Uzi appeared before the Cuban. The Uzi crackled, and a stream of slugs whistled close to Encizo.

After that things became a blur.

Encizo, bearing in mind what Katz had said about the contact man, didn't dare fire for fear of hitting anyone who might be deeper inside the panel truck. At the same time, he was aware that something had to be done quickly in order to reduce the threat of the gunman who had burst from the truck.

And the fiery Cuban acted, more from reflex than anything else. He used his MP-5 as a club, slashing the hard barrel across the gunman's right knee. The blow was hard, delivered with every ounce of Encizo's power behind it, and Encizo himself heard the knee-cap break. The gunman let out a squeal of agony, falling forward from the rear of the truck as his injured leg gave way under his weight. He plunged out of the truck, crashing headfirst to the road, his Uzi spilling from his fingers as he struck. Encizo followed through, reversing the MP-5 and whacking it across the back of the downed gunman's skull.

With the crackle of autofire in the air, Katz yanked open the driver's door. He thrust the muzzle of his Uzi before him as he peered into the cab of the panel truck. The first thing he saw was the bound and gagged figure lying in a crumpled heap on the floor on the passenger's side of the cab. His attention was drawn from the figure as a dark shape lunged over the back of the seat. Katz caught a glimmer of light as it lanced along the barrel of a handgun. He ducked, and immediately heard the slam of a shot and felt it whiz close by. The bullet crashed through the windshield, blowing shattered glass onto the road. Staying low, Katz turned the muzzle of the Uzi against the padded backrest of the seat and pulled the trigger, sending a short burst of 9 mm slugs through the upholstery and into the lower torso of the man who had just tried to kill him. The guy let out a long screech of pain as the slugs burned through him. He arched back, slamming to the floor of the panel truck, then lay there writhing in pain.

"Everybody okay?" McCarter called into the silence that followed the final shots of the short, frantic encounter.

"Fine back here," Encizo called as he hauled his prisoner to his feet. The Guatemalan was moaning, indicating he was unable to walk properly due to his injured knee. Encizo spoke to him in rapid Spanish, telling him that if he didn't walk, and fast, much worse would happen to him. The Guatemalan, grumbling vociferously, hobbled around to the front of the panel truck. "Cal, give me a hand," Katz said.

James opened the passenger door and saw the bound figure on the floor of the cab. With Katz's help he eased the man out of the vehicle. Drawing his Jet Aer knife, the black Phoenix warrior cut the ropes, then he removed the thick gag drawn tightly over the victim's mouth.

The man gulped in air, coughing harshly. Then gingerly he started to rub his wrists where the ropes had gouged his flesh.

"Jesus, am I glad you guys turned up when you did," he said. "I'm José Rios."

"What got you into this mess?" McCarter asked.

Rios smiled a little sheepishly. "My own big mouth, I guess. I did some checking for Washington on their suggestion that there might be Russians in the area. They were pushing for answers because of this Soviet pilot coming down with his fancy jet, so I did the same. I must have pushed too hard. After I got the call to meet you guys, I took off. When I got here, this bunch showed up and jumped me. It appears they trailed me all the way in. Figured I had to be meeting somebody if I was sitting out here, so they took over."

"After you'd given them the wrong identification signals?" James said.

"No way I was going to make it easy for the mothers," Rios replied.

McCarter, who had finished securing the captives with plastic riot cuffs, glanced at the agent. "Who are these charmers? Local guerrillas?"

"This bunch? Guerrillas?" Rios's dark face creased into a wide smile. "Nah, all these boys can claim is that they're bandits. Smugglers. Border jumpers. Local Mafia is all, and not too bright when it comes to adding two plus two."

"So, why interfere with you?" Encizo asked.

"These creeps would interfere with anybody and anything if they smelled profit. Also, I know for a fact that they've run guns and supplies in for the Communists. When they heard me asking around for information, they could have figured that if they could take me and whoever I was meeting, maybe they could trade us all off for a price. These boys never miss a trick."

"Rios, do they have a base where they operate from?" Katz asked.

The agent nodded. "There's a village to the east. Maybe an hour's drive. They have their HQ there."

"Could be the place to get us some answers," Katz said.

The dead bandits were placed in the back of the panel truck with their surviving partners sitting over them. Katz sat next to the Rios in the front of the truck, with the others on the rear seat.

"Let's go, Rios," Katz ordered. "The one thing we don't have a lot of is time. Everything hinges on how fast we can get information and act on it."

"Hang on, guys, 'cause this track ain't nothing like the L.A. Freeway," the agent warned, then stomped his foot down on the gas pedal. The panel truck lurched forward, picking up speed rapidly. The engine was noisy, blowing clouds of smoke from its exhaust, but the truck also picked up speed so suddenly on the uneven terrain that it even shook the confidence of an experienced driver like McCarter.

"Bloody hell," he muttered. "If the bandits don't get us, this damn truck will!"

8

Gary Manning was awakened by the tramping of heavy boots outside the hut where he had spent the night. It had been an uncomfortable experience, not only due to the roughness of the building, but also because Manning had been tied to a wooden seat and left there. Since arriving at the hidden base of Salazar's band late in the afternoon of the previous day, Manning had been left totally alone in the hut. He had heard activity outside the hut and had been able to catch glimpses of movement through cracks in the wall. Otherwise he had been ignored.

The treatment hadn't worried Manning. He knew it was deliberate, an attempt to unsettle him and to place fears in his mind. He was supposed to worry and fret, to imagine that his captives were devising all kinds of terrible things to do to him. Which may have been true, for all he knew. If so, there wasn't a damn thing he could do about it. On the psychological side Gary Manning was not worried at all. If Kirov thought that the silent treatment was going to unhinge the Canadian's mind, then the Spetsnaz officer needed to go back to the manual.

What did concern Manning was the fate of Ilya Roskov. Before he had been shoved into the hut,

Manning had seen Roskov being escorted into a similar hut some distance away. He hoped that the young Soviet pilot was simply being held captive until the arrival of some form of transport that would return him to Russia. The Phoenix warrior hoped that no ill treatment had befallen the defecting flyer. The Soviets were capable of meting out harsh punishment to those of their kind who turned their backs on Mother Russia.

Manning's somber thoughts vanished as the door to the hut swung open and Captain Kirov entered, followed by an armed Spetsnaz trooper. The trooper positioned himself beside the door as Kirov closed it.

"Before you ask," Manning said, "I did not sleep well."

Kirov peered at the Canadian, the faintest glimmer of a smile touching his lips. "Your presence here is a source of embarrassment," the Russian explained.

Manning found he had to grin despite his predicament. "Since when have Spetsnaz been natives of Guatemala?" he asked.

But Kirov wasn't willing to be baited, and he merely shrugged. "We are all here on sufferance," he said. "As far as I am concerned, my presence is preferable to yours. However, my main concern must be directed toward establishing how much information you have on our involvement here."

Manning said nothing. He understood Kirov's implications. The Soviet involvement with the local guerrillas was a delicate affair. From Kirov's reactions it seemed evident that there was a need for the Russians to maintain their low-profile presence.

For a fleeting moment Manning imagined the knowledge offering him some kind of bargaining power. Along the lines of "I won't tell about you if you let me go." He dismissed the thought instantly, embarrassed at his own naïveté. The Russian would have simply laughed in his face if he had brought the subject up. Kirov did not need to bargain. He already held the winning hand. All aces, and he simply had to play them at his own convenience.

As if he had read the Canadian's mind, Kirov said, "I could dispose of you at any time." He was clearly letting Manning know how precarious his position was. "On the other hand, I could keep you alive and send you back to Moscow along with the traitor Roskov."

"Except if...?" Manning queried.

Kirov managed a full smile this time. "Except if you give me the answers I require."

"All I'd be doing would be lengthening my term of imprisonment," Manning said.

"You would be alive."

"You mean in a psycho ward in some Soviet hospital for undesirables, or a labor camp. Some choice."

"But still alive," Kirov persisted. "Would you actually prefer an early death? Do you hate us so much? What is that American phrase? Yes, I remember. 'Better dead than Red!'"

"I still have nothing to say."

Kirov paced the floor, hands clasped behind his back. Abruptly he stopped. "You leave me no choice." He turned and barked an order in Russian to the guard.

The Spetsnaz turned and left. Kirov sat down behind the trestle table that stood on the far side of the room. He bit the end off a thin black cigar he produced from a pocket in his camou fatigues and proceeded to light it. He sat smoking, regarding Manning with cold, dead eyes.

A few minutes later the guard returned, accompanied by a tough-looking Spetsnaz who had a distinctly unfriendly attitude. The moment Manning locked eyes with him, he knew things were about to go from bad to indescribably terrible.

Kirov spoke to the newcomer, who listened with interest, then made a brief comment of his own before crossing the room to confront Manning.

The Spetsnaz sized the Canadian up with a practiced eye. He had obviously done this kind of thing before, and Manning knew that he would be thorough and extremely proficient.

Kirov got up, as though to make a casual introduction. "This is Karamatsov," he announced. "I will let him speak for himself."

The introduction took the form of Karamatsov's right fist crashing against Manning's jaw. The blow was hard, but not too hard. It whipped Manning's head sideways with a vicious snap, numbing the lower half of his face. His back teeth cut into the soft flesh of his mouth, and he tasted blood. He was still reeling from the blow when Karamatsov took hold of his hair and yanked his head around to the front. For a fleeting moment the two men stared into each other's eyes. Karamatsov's features wavered before Manning's gaze, and he never even saw the second blow coming. He felt it, though. There was an explosion of silent pain, and blood sprayed from his slack mouth as his head rocked backward. Manning strained against the bonds holding him to the seat even though he knew struggle was useless. He raged silently in his frustration because there was nothing else he could do. His wild anger was a thin barrier against the pain that he had experienced and what was yet to come. And come it did. The silent Karamatsov devoted his energy to delivering blow after blow to Manning's face and body, each designed to inflict pain without causing an injury that might prove fatal. After the first few minutes Manning's face had become a bloody mask, flesh gashed and bruised by the pounding fists. His ribs burned with pain from the hammering they had received. The beating seemed endless as the slam of fists against flesh became repetitive.

And then silence descended.

It took some time for Manning to realize that the beating had stopped. He was slumped over in the seat. He'd managed to maintain his position on the chair only because of the restraining ropes. He was staring at the floor of the hut, at his own feet, and it dawned on him suddenly that the dark splashes on the floor and on his boots had been caused by the blood dripping from his face. He forced himself upright, ignoring the stabs of pain, finding that he could only see through his right eye. The other was swollen shut. He had to blink several times before he could focus with his good eye. As the room swam into view, he became aware of the two Russians watching him.

"Very good," Kirov said. "You have recovered much faster than I expected."

"Just what do you hope to achieve?" Manning asked through cut and bleeding lips.

"I want you to tell me whether I need to worry about being overrun by more of your comrades. Or you can convince me that you came in alone and have not had the opportunity to tell your people of our presence." Kirov gestured impatiently. "Even you have to accept that I am not asking a great deal."

"If you asked me the time of day, it would be too much," Manning mumbled.

Kirov sighed. "I had the feeling you were going to say something like that. You understand, of course, that your reluctance in imparting any information you have will only prolong your suffering. Karamatsov can continue this interrogation for a long time. He has used only the crudest method up to now. I am sure you are aware that there are other ways of inflicting pain. Ways that will make what has just happened feel like a woman's kiss. Let me assure you, my friend, that Karamatsov enjoys his work. He has studied his subject well. He excels when it comes to things that cut and burn, and I promise you that he will use these methods if you persist in maintaining this stupidly stubborn resistance."

Manning held the Russian's gaze, saying nothing.

Karamatsov turned to Kirov, and the two men spoke in low tones. Then the Spetsnaz commander nodded, and Karamatsov turned and left the hut.

"We are going to give you a little time to think matters over. Reflect on the price you may have to pay for your bovine loyalty. And all for nothing, because at the end of the day you will tell me what I want to know. *That I promise.*"

With that he, too, left the hut, taking the guard with him. Manning was left alone with his thoughts and his pain.

CROSSING THE COMPOUND outside the hut, Kirov found his train of thought diverted by the appearance of Salazar. The guerrilla leader obviously had something on his mind. He hurried across to confront the Spetsnaz commander.

"Three of my men left last night," Salazar said. "I have only just been told."

"Deserted?" Kirov asked.

Salazar shook his head. "No. They have gone looking for their comrade who fell over the edge of the trail with the American. They believe you were wrong not to allow them to look for him when the accident took place."

"So now they will waste time looking for a dead man?"

"He may not be dead," Salazar protested. "What if he is injured, alone and unable to move?"

"Then he soon will be dead," Kirov replied. "We have far more important things to concern us, Salazar. You should know that."

"For myself I accept what you say. But these men have been together for a long time. They are like brothers. When one is hurt, they all bleed. I cannot fault them for their loyalty."

"It is done now," Kirov said. "You handle it how you wish."

"What will we be doing today?"

"Later we will go over the procedure for setting the explosives and the timing mechanism. But first I must make contact with the *Pushkin*. I need to know how soon the retrieval squad will arrive. When we finally have Roskov and that damn plane off our hands, I will feel much better.''

9

Rios concealed the truck a mile away from the village, pointing out that it was advisable for them to complete the journey on foot. "We drive in and they're going to know we're coming," he said. "And believe me, they would be waiting for us. This way at least we have a chance to catch them unaware."

"Makes sense," James agreed.

"Who's the main man?" Encizo asked.

"A real slimeball—name of Jorge," Rios said. "This guy is so crooked his shadow has a hunchback."

"You ever meet him?" James asked.

"Once. My cover has been as a dealer in questionable goods. I did a deal with him over a shipment of hijacked Scotch. Gave me the time to look round the village and fix the layout in my head for future reference."

"Where did the Scotch come from?" McCarter asked.

Rios grinned. "U.S. government bonded warehouse."

"All in the name of national security," James commented.

"Hell, it's all down to buying and selling," Rios said. "Nobody wants to part with information for nothing. Down here everybody trades."

"Will your cover be blown now?" Katz asked.

Rios nodded. "I guess so."

"Hey, that's bad, man," James sympathized. "How long have you worked this assignment?"

"I've been down here nearly three years," Rios said. "The day had to come when my luck ran out. I've been lucky. What the hell—it will be good to get home for a stretch."

"Where's home?"

"East L.A.," Rios answered. "My old man runs a fruit and vegetable store. Whenever I get back, I help him behind the counter."

He slid an Uzi SMG from its clip beneath the driver's seat, checking the magazine. He slipped a few spare mags into the inside pocket of his leather jacket.

The deep-cover operative led the Force through the dense, humid forest with the assurance of a man who knows his territory and is at ease with his surroundings. Rios, during his three-year stint in Guatemala, had absorbed the feel of the land and its native culture. He was no longer acting the part—he had become as one with it.

When they neared their target, Rios called a halt. Under his direction the Force deployed along a grassy rise from where they could observe the activities in the village.

Calling the place a village was being generous. It consisted of a cluster of adobe buildings. There was a stone-walled well in an area that appeared to function as a plaza. Trash littered the ground, along with the wrecks of two old military-type trucks. A general air of neglect hung over the place. There was little movement at that early hour. Smoke rose from the chimneys of a number of the huts, and a few chickens wandered about aimlessly, pecking at the ground. From its spot against the wall of one hut, a dog rose stiffly, stretching its legs and body as it moved.

"One thing for certain," McCarter observed. "That dump will never get on the cover of *Ideal Homes*."

"Jorge and his bunch of scuzzballs aren't exactly housetrained," Rios said. "This bunch is strictly lower than lowlife."

"So how do we handle this?" Encizo asked. "Let's face it—we're obviously not going to be welcome in there."

"Maybe we should hit 'em hard and fast. Don't give them time to organize," Calvin James suggested. "With luck, most of them could still be asleep."

"Could work," Katz remarked. "Rios, what sort of numbers are we talking about?"

"No more than fifteen, sixteen," Rios estimated. "At times there are a few women around the place. Jorge only has them around for menial work and to keep his men happy."

"These guys," McCarter asked. "Are they seasoned fighters?"

Rios shook his head. "They are ragtag bandits, not guerrillas. Don't get me wrong—they can handle weapons all right, but they're not specialists. You had a taste when you went up against those boys who jumped me."

"One thing we have to remember," James pointed out. "These guys are on their own turf, and the odds are on their side."

"Just my kind of setup," McCarter remarked.

Katz, who had been studying the layout, turned to Rios.

"Where would we be likely to find Jorge?"

Rios indicated a building larger than the rest, with a roofed porch running its length. "That's where he'll be."

"You sound confident about that," Encizo remarked.

"Only because I know he's there," the agent said. "See the pole in front of the building? The flag is flying. That means Jorge is at home. The guy believes he's some kind of military genius. Likes to play the game to the hilt."

"Okay," Katz said. "We go in. Aim for that building and try to grab Jorge alive. He's our target. We need information fast. We have to locate where those Spetsnaz are holding our people and Roskov before they ship them out—or worse."

Katz and Encizo moved off first, slipping over the grassy ridge to work their way in toward the closest adobe hut. McCarter, James and Rios edged along the ridge for a few yards before making their approach.

A door creaked, and a man stepped out into the warmth of the early sun. He screwed up his eyes against the brightness, staring around him as he scrubbed his hands through his tangled hair. He wore grubby pants and an unbuttoned shirt. A Kalashnikov hung from his shoulder by a leather sling.

Somebody called out from inside the hut, and he replied over his shoulder. As the summons came again, he began to turn, his head swinging around slowly, eyes looking out toward the slope beyond the village. He had already started to reply when his words died.

He focused his eyes on the slope. A startled cry burst from his throat.

There were armed men moving in on the village!

The man snatched for the AK-47 and began to yell at the top of his voice.

10

"Bloody hell!" David McCarter couldn't believe their bad luck—being spotted on the final stretch.

He heard the yell of alarm and saw the guy unsling the AK-47 he was carrying. The man brought the weapon to bear and opened fire without hesitation.

The ground in front of McCarter and James and Rios erupted in a series of dirt spouts as the 7.62 mm slugs struck, forcing the three of them to scatter in defense.

James raised his M-16 and triggered a 3-round burst. His bullets whacked the adobe to one side of the target's head. Chips of adobe stung the back of the bandit's neck, causing him to slacken his finger against the trigger.

The distraction gave McCarter the opportunity to make a concentrated dash for the hut. His long legs pumped furiously, driving the British warrior at full tilt.

Catching sight of McCarter's headlong approach, the Guatemalan turned his Kalashnikov toward him, triggering wildly as he caught a glimpse of McCarter's wild expression. The AK-47 rattled harshly, spitting a hellish string of 7.62 mm slugs in McCarter's direction.

McCarter hit the ground in a long dive. Bullets slashed air above his hurtling form. If he had been a split second slower, the British ace would already have been history. A tremor of fear climbed his spine, but the excitement of the battlefield was greater than his terror. The fear was part of that excitement. Adrenaline rushed through McCarter to add speed to his motions as he shoulder-rolled across the ground. More bullets tore into the earth near his body as McCarter threw out his booted feet and came to a sudden halt.

He lay on his back and spotted the enemy gunman. The figure was in a kneeling stance by a tree trunk. He had started to shift the aim of his weapon to try to track McCarter's rolling figure and nail him with another burst of lead messengers. The guy hadn't expected the Briton to stop suddenly in midroll. As he tried to adjust his aim, McCarter's KG-99 spit fire. Shooting overhead from a prone position on his back, the Phoenix pro relied on years of training and instincts as he fired the subgun in this unconventional manner. The Guatemalan dropped his weapon as three 9 mm parabellums slammed into his chest. The man collapsed against the tree and slid lifeless to the ground.

James and Rios ran to the first hut. As they cleared the front wall, a pair of armed opponents appeared from another dwelling. The black commando jumped to cover and pushed the Company man out of the line of fire a split second before one of the gunmen opened fire with a full-auto weapon. Bullets stitched the adobe, ripping chunks from the corner inches from James's bowed head. The former SWAT cop took a grenade from his belt and pulled the pin. He leaned away from the corner of the wall as more bullets slammed into the shelter. James popped the spoon to the grenade and counted to two before he flung the miniblaster at the enemy pair.

"¡Granada!" a voice cried out in warning. One of the gunmen had spotted James's nasty little present.

The explosion closely followed the man's warning. Dust spewed from the blast and swirled into a cloud between the huts. James gestured for Rios to provide support as he broke cover to check on the enemy. One thug had been torn apart by the grenade blast. The other had been thrown against the adobe wall of a hut. He sat with his back to the wall, both legs mangled and bloodied by shrapnel. Although blood stained his shirtfront, the man still held a submachine gun in his lap and started to raise it when he saw Calvin James. The Phoenix warrior had no choice. He snap-aimed the M-16 and triggered a 3 round burst. The 5.56 mm projectiles bored into the man's torso and blasted a hole in his heart. As James saw the dead man slide to the ground, he gestured for Rios to come forward.

"Oh, man!" the CIA agent groaned when he saw the blood-splattered remains of the slain bandits. Rios felt he was about to throw up.

"Come on," James urged as he grabbed Rios's arm. "You can puke when we get to cover."

The Phoenix tough guy jogged to the next adobe hut and towed Rios by the arm for a moment or two until he was certain the agent was moving in the right direction. The sounds of battle in the village would assure him that Rios kept moving. The firefight was far from over, and they had to keep going, use cover and stay alert until it was finished.

SO MUCH FOR THE ELEMENT of surprise, Katz thought when he heard the first shots. There was no time to dwell on it. Analyzing the reasons why something went wrong in a combat situation is something best done after the event, not during it.

Katz and Encizo rushed toward another hut. The door opened, and a fat, sweating bandit appeared. He was brandishing an AK-47 and yelling in a loud voice. Without breaking his stride, and moving with surprising agility for someone of his bulk, the bandit ran directly toward Encizo. The AK-47 swung up and began to fire. Bullets hissed through the air around Encizo, some dangerously close. But the enemy had made one of the classic errors of combat. He hadn't assessed the distance between himself and his target, and on top of it he had also tried to fire while on the move. Both were common faults and received the kind of response they deserved.

Encizo dropped to one knee, the MP-5 tracking the bandit for a few seconds. Then the Cuban touched the trigger to return fire, blasting a stream of 9 mm death in the direction of the sweating man. The guy's dirty shirtfront bloomed red flowers as the slugs bit deep into his chest. He threw his arms into the air in a gesture of despair, then toppled over onto his back.

Katz found himself under fire from a guy shooting through a window. Although the bullets chewed up the ground at his feet, the Israeli turned in the direction of the gunman, raising his Uzi. With the barrel resting across his steel prosthesis, Katz took aim and fired. The Uzi stuttered loudly, sending 9 mm slugs howling across the intervening space. The first few blew chunks out of the adobe, then as Katz slightly adjusted his aim, the following burst caught the sniper full in the face. He uttered a strangled cry as his features dissolved under the crushing impact of the bullets, and fell back into the room in agony.

Returning the fire that was suddenly being directed at them from all angles, Katz and Encizo ducked and weaved their way through the haphazard collection of adobe huts. Despite the delays caused by constant engagement with the opposition, they negotiated the greater part of the distance—then found themselves pinned down against the wall of one hut.

"To hell with this!" Encizo muttered as his H&K snapped on an empty chamber. He tossed the weapon aside and snatched a fragmentation grenade from his combat harness. Pulling the pin, the Cuban powerhouse flung the sphere in the direction of a trio of half-dressed bandits who were advancing on the Phoenix pair.

The blast of the grenade tossed one guy six feet in the air, his lacerated body glistening red. The other two suffered less traumatic effects, but were wounded enough to keep them out of the firefight for the duration.

Even as the dust from the explosion was still rising, Encizo snatched up his MP-5 and slotted in a fresh magazine. He cocked the weapon and turned to glance at Katz.

"You ready to go for it?" he asked.

Katz nodded as he finished replacing a magazine in the Uzi. "Come on," he said, "I want that Jorge."

He broke cover, sprinting across the open space toward the large hut. Bullets whacked the ground around Katz. He ran for the main building and fired his Uzi at the enemy position. The Phoenix commander sprayed 9 mm bullets in a volley designed to keep the bandits preoccupied with staying alive rather than actually trying to hit a target. Enzizo added cover fire with his H&K chopper as Katz dashed to a corner of the building for shelter.

The Israeli swapped magazines to the Uzi to be certain he had ample firepower and nodded to Enzizo. The Cuban warrior resisted the urge to cross himself and charged into the open. Katz poked the stubby barrel of the Uzi around the corner and fired another hail of parabellums. The covering fire forced those bandits foolish enough to show themselves to have a change of heart and duck out of sight. Enzizo blasted his MP-5 at the enemy as he sprinted to Katz's position.

Katz jerked his prosthesis toward the door to the building. The Cuban moved to one side, and Katz stood at the other. The Israeli stayed clear of the door, in case an opponent inside decided to shoot through it, and slammed a boot just below the doorknob. The door swung open and no shots responded. Enzizo crouched low and propelled himself inside while Katz covered him from the doorway.

The Cuban entered a large room. Wooden packing cases stood stacked high in one corner, and a cluttered workbench was set against the opposite wall. Directly ahead of Enzizo was an open door. The light from the doorway was blocked by a figure armed with a pump shotgun.

The bandit pointed his weapon at Enzizo, but suddenly glimpsed Katz at the entrance. He adjusted the aim of the 12-gauge blaster just as Katz's Uzi triggered a short burst. Bullets chewed the doorway near the shotgunner, but the bandit dropped low in time to avoid being hit by the Uzi slugs.

Encizo had rushed to the stack of crates for cover. He trained his H&K on the enemy gunman and fired a trio of parabellums. The bandit's skull split open from the impact of two high-velocity 124-grain projectiles. His twitching finger triggered the shotgun, and a blast of buckshot smashed into the crates near Encizo's position. The Cuban sucked air through clenched teeth as he heard Double-O-Buck pellets splinter wood inches from his head.

A shape moved near Encizo, and he started to swing the H&K subgun toward the potential threat. The Cuban recognized Katz and raised the barrel toward the ceiling. He sighed with relief. Katz glanced at the still shape at the doorway. The condition of his head, or what was left of it, assured him the man no longer presented a threat. Encizo approached the doorway and carefully peered at the passage beyond. A number of doors stood at the walls of the corridor.

"This place is bigger than it looks from the outside," the Cuban muttered as Katz moved beside him.

"Big enough for the rest of the bandits to hold out in," Katz stated, and braced the Uzi across his artificial limb. "We can't assume we got them all when we exchanged fire with them on the way here."

"I hope we didn't get them all," Encizo commented. "Jorge is worth more to us alive."

They ventured into the passage. Encizo kicked in the first door to find a food store. The next led to a crude kitchen. A steaming coffee pot was suspended over an open cook fire burning in the stone hearth. The kitchen was deserted, but a loud snap drew Encizo's attention to a corner by an ice trap. Movement on the floor startled the Cuban and he grunted with surprise when he saw a fat brown rat thrashing about with the steel bow of a big trap across its neck. The locking bar and wood base scraped the floor as the rat convulsed in the final throes of death.

Gunfire rattled at the far end of the passage. Katz and Encizo rushed through the corridor toward the sound and reached the last door. Katz kicked it open.

They stepped into a large, low-ceilinged room that apparently served as both living and sleeping quarters. There was a large brass bed under one window, containing crumpled sheets and blankets that hadn't been washed in years. Beat-up furniture was scattered around the room. Various items of clothing occupied the floor, vying for space with empty beer cans, food wrappers and cigar butts. The air smelled stale, reeking of unwashed bodies and overcooked food.

Two dead bandits lay on the floor, blood seeping from their punctured flesh.

McCarter, James and Rios stood in a loose formation around a large, heavy-muscled man in filthy olive fatigues. Thick black hair hung around his broad, brown face. The man was not frightened despite his situation. His bright black eyes darted around the room, assessing his captors.

Rios announced, "Gentlemen, meet Jorge. Bandit and scumbag."

The bandit leader turned his gaze on Rios, and his fleshy lips pulled into a sneer. "And you are a damn Yankee spy," he said in heavily accented English. "I must be getting old to have been fooled by such as you."

"Tut-tut," McCarter chided. "If there's one thing I can't stomach, it's a bad loser."

"Rios, you stay with me," Katz said. "The rest of you check the area. Make sure we got all the bandits."

"Right," McCarter replied, and glared at Jorge. "Give a yell if you want me to help you to get this bastard to talk."

The Briton, Encizo and James left to check the area and to take a few more prisoners who had stuck their shirts on their rifles to indicate surrender. Jorge eyed the middle-aged, one-armed Israeli with open contempt. Katz took a pack of Camels from a shirt pocket and shook a cigarette loose. He adroitly plucked it from the pack with the hooks of his prosthesis.

"An aging cripple is the best the Yankee government can do?" the bandit remarked with a sneer.

"We went through your men without much trouble, and you're our prisoner, Jorge," Katz said with a smile. "It seems we're good enough. There's no time for small talk or chitchat. We're going to ask some questions, and you'll answer them."

"What if I refuse?" Jorge inquired.

Katz lighted his cigarette with a Ronson and blew smoke at the bandit.

"Imagine the most terrible things that could happen to your body," the Israeli answered quietly. "We'll come up with something worse."

Rios gulped and stared at Katz. He didn't know the Phoenix commander was bluffing. Phoenix Force wouldn't use torture—not only because it was impractical and unreliable, but because it was also immoral. Jorge looked away from Katz. He was rattled and clearly believed the threat to be genuine.

"Hey, wait a minute," Rios began as he approached Katz. "I don't want anything to do with torture...."

He stepped between Katz and Jorge. Rios even had his back to the bandit leader. Katz moved in to pull Rios away from Jorge, but the desperate man had already seen his opportunity and attacked.

Jorge grabbed Rios from behind and wrapped an arm around his throat as he smashed a knee to the CIA man's tailbone. Rios groaned and bent backward. Jorge quickly plucked a Ka-Bar military Bowie knife from a sheath on Rios's belt. Katz charged forward to stop the bandit. Jorge suddenly released Rios and pushed him into the Israeli.

The impact struck the Uzi from Katz's grasp. He let the subgun fall and tried to get around Rios to jump Jorge before the bandit could use the knife. A shriek of agony announced that he was too late. Jorge had plunged the blade between Rios's shoulder blades. He yanked the knife free as Katz closed in.

Jorge raised the bloodied blade, and the Israeli's prosthesis streaked forward to clamp the steel hooks around the wrist above the knife. His left fist hooked a hard punch to Jorge's jaw as he twisted the captured wrist in his metal talons. Bones popped, and the bandit screamed as his wrist seemed to snap in two. The knife fell from his trembling fingers as Katz bent his left arm and delivered a front elbow-smash to his opponent's face.

The bandit started to stumble, blood oozing from his mouth and nostrils. Yet he managed to throw a roundhouse punch at Katz. The prosthesis rose to block it, and Katz chopped the side of his hand across Jorge's collarbone. The blow doubled up Jorge, and his face bobbed low to receive a powerful knee-kick. The bandit leader buckled to the floor.

"Medic!" Katz shouted as he glanced at José Rios. Blood poured from the deep stab wound between the fallen man's shoulder blades.

Calvin James and David McCarter were already at the door. They had heard Rios scream when he was stabbed, and had rushed back to the room. James immediately hurried to Rios and ripped open the back of the agent's shirt. He reached for his medical kit and shook his head grimly.

"Jesus," the black warrior rasped. "It looks bad. I think he got it **in the** spine. Might have hit the lung, too."

McCarter turned from Rios to fix a furious stare at Jorge. The bandit slowly started to rise, one hand cupped over his bloodied mouth and broken nose. The British ace stomped forward and lashed a vicious kick to Jorge's ribs. The man squealed in pain and fell back to the floor.

"Get up, you filthy bastard!" McCarter snarled. "I'll take you outside and kick your arse until you're wearing it around your neck!"

"That's enough!" Katz snapped. "I know how you feel, but back off... *for now*."

The Briton moved away from Jorge and scooped up the blood-stained Ka-Bar knife. The bandit sat on the floor, nursing his broken wrist and wiping blood from his face with a sleeve. McCarter displayed an unpleasant smile that would have seemed at home on the face of a lunatic in a straitjacket. He stepped toward Jorge and waved the knife in his fist so the bandit would see the crimson smear on the blade.

"Rios's blood," McCarter announced. "Yours will be on this knife next, Jorge. I'm going to whittle on you for a long while. You'll be begging me to kill you..."

"Not yet," Katz insisted. "You don't carve him up unless he refuses to talk. Then we'll all get to work on him."

Jorge's eyes swelled with fear. McCarter displayed another crazy grin and marched to where James was trying to do the best he could for Rios. Katz retrieved his Uzi and glanced at the Briton. McCarter had put on a good act. At least, Katz was pretty sure most of it was an act.

"You'd better cooperate," Katz told the bandit.

"How do I know you won't kill me even if I do talk?" Jorge asked.

"We're not murderers," Katz answered. "If you do what we say and answer our questions, we'll let you live. Reluctantly, but we'll let you live."

"Do I have your word of honor?" Jorge demanded.

"Where did a bucket of garbage like you come across the word 'honor'?" McCarter snarled.

"Man, I can use some help here," James told McCarter. He gave Rios an injection of morphine as he spoke. "See if you can get me some hot water and strips of cloth to serve as bandages. I don't have enough in my kit to bind him up well enough. I can't promise it'll do any good anyway."

"I'll see what I can do," McCarter replied grimly as he turned and left the room.

"*Señor*." Jorge directed the question to Katz. "Your word?"

"You have my word that none of my men nor myself will kill you or torture, mutilate or otherwise injure you if you answer our questions," the Phoenix commander replied with a nod. "That is, of course, if you tell us the truth. Fair enough?"

"All right," Jorge said. "What do you want to know?"

11

It was light when Jack Grimaldi opened his eyes. He lay still for a few minutes, then slowly started easing the stiffness out of his body. And he was plenty bruised. His body felt tender, his ribs ached, making him catch his breath if he stretched too quickly. He knew it was going to take time for the soreness to go away. In the meantime he had to move and clear out from the area in case someone came looking for him. What he needed to do was to get back to Dragon Slayer. If he could get the combat chopper back in the air, then it was going to take more than a squad of Spetsnaz heavies to stop him.

Grimaldi was also sane enough to accept that it wasn't going to be that easy. He hadn't forgotten that there were Spetsnaz and Guatemalan guerrillas guarding the helicopter and Roskov's jet.

The Stony Man flyer eased to his feet. The heat of the day soaked into his body, helping to drive some of the stiffness from his joints. First things first, he decided. There was the matter of the guerrilla who had gone over the edge with him. Was the guy still alive, maybe wandering around looking for Grimaldi? He wasn't forgetting the fact that the guerrilla had been armed with an AK-47.

Grimaldi scouted the immediate area, returning by a circuitous route to the place where he had found himself after the fall. He viewed the place from a thicket of huge ferns, still able to see the scattering of broken branches and foliage that had come down with him.

So, where had the other guy landed? It had to be reasonably close. The problem was the heavy undergrowth. It was so dense in places that it would have been no trouble to hide a damn truck. Grimaldi sat back on his heels, scanning the surroundings methodically. Even so, he almost missed the telltale gleam of metal the first time around, but something tugged at the back of his mind, drawing his gaze to the spot again. Grimaldi fixed the position in his mind, zeroing in on it. He studied it for long minutes, ignoring the insects that began to gather around him. The rising heat of the day was starting to make him sweat. His shirt stuck to his back, and perspiration dampened his face, making his unshaven skin itch.

Finally he decided to go take a closer look. Once again he approached the spot slowly and by a roundabout route. It took time, but Grimaldi figured it was better to take half an hour in this life than spend eternity regretting haste in the next.

When he did reach the object, he was sorry. The gleaming metal was the blade of a knife that had slipped from its sheath to become wedged in a fork of a branch. The knife had belonged to the guerrilla who had fallen over the edge of the trail with Grimaldi. Fate, however, had not been too kind to the Guatemalan rebel. His descent had been halted by an upthrusting section of a broken branch. The jagged spear of wood had impaled the guerrilla, almost tearing his upper body in half. There was an awful lot of blood and viscera, which had attracted hordes of flies and other jungle creatures.

Grimaldi cast around for the dead man's weapon. After a five-minute search he found it nestled in a bed of ferns. The AK-47 had suffered little damage in the fall. Grimaldi checked the magazine and found it to be full. He also inspected the autorifle's mechanism and judged it satisfactory. Returning to the grisly corpse, Grimaldi retrieved the knife and used it to cut free the combat harness the guerrilla had been wearing. There were three spare magazines for the Kalashnikov in the pouches. Grimaldi took these and distributed them among the large pockets in his combat trousers.

There was nothing else of use he could gain from the dead man. Grimaldi moved out. He had already worked out his position by the movement of the sun, aware that he needed to be heading to the west. That would take him back toward the coast. And somewhere between his present position and the Pacific Ocean was Dragon Slayer.

There was no point in searching for a trail that might lead him back to the helicopter. The walk in from the landing point had been through dense jungle. There were no paths or real landmarks. So Grimaldi used his navigational skills to at least put him in an approximately right direction.

He had been pushing his way through the lush greenery, sweating profusely, for almost two hours when he got the feeling that he wasn't alone.

Grimaldi didn't panic. He continued moving forward, but imperceptibly slowed his rate of travel. The sensation of being followed grew stronger, but as yet he hadn't seen or heard anything. That didn't change his mind, though, because he was working from an inner feeling that kept nagging away at him. It was a small, silent voice that told him there was someone on his trail. He'd acquired the capability from years of living by his wits and of experiencing day-by-day scenarios much like the one he now found himself in. Grimaldi had served his time in the battlefields, and he *knew* when he was being tracked.

He broke through the crowding mass of vegetation and found himself on the edge of a clearing. Just ahead of him was a placid, swampy pool some twenty feet long by at least ten feet across. Insects hovered above the still water. On the far side the tangled undergrowth rustled as an unseen creature moved to the edge of the pool to drink.

Grimaldi slowed his stride, debating which way to go.

At that moment an autorifle crackled. Bullets whipped through the foliage to the left of his body.

Grimaldi broke to the right, ducking low as he headed for cover, skirting the edge of the pool. He could hear voices now. At least two of them, maybe more. His ears picked up the sound of bodies rushing through the undergrowth. He cut off to the right, plunging into thick undergrowth and ignoring the slash of thin branches whipping back against his face. He pushed in deep, on hands and knees, sinking into the spongy mass of the forest floor.

He could hear his trackers clearly now, and moments later was able to see them as they reached the clearing. Grimaldi studied them and realized after a few seconds that he knew at least one of their faces. The one he recognized had been part of the guerrilla band that had captured Grimaldi, Manning and Ilya Roskov.

So they had come looking for him, after all—or maybe they had been searching for their dead partner. He wondered whether they had found him.

The guerrillas moved farther into the open. Grimaldi withdrew farther into the undergrowth, hugging the AK-47 close to his body.

The three guerrillas halted in the clearing, right on the edge of the pool, and peered about intently. They were arguing between themselves without letup, each man trying to force his opinion on the others. One, with a stronger personality than his companions, demanded they concentrate their search in the immediate area. He was convinced their quarry was close by. His insistence paid off, and despite their misgivings, the other two fell in with his demands.

Spreading out, the guerrillas began a thorough search.

Grimaldi curled his finger around the AK-47's trigger, knowing that the numbers were falling and he was going to have to fight his way out of this situation. There was no way he could slip away without being noticed. With near-impenetrable jungle at his back, the only way to go was forward, and the guerrillas had him between *them* and freedom.

The Stony Man flyer considered the odds and came to the conclusion that an offensive maneuver would tip the scales in his favor. He had no doubts in his mind that the guerrillas had him tagged as a shoot-on-sight target. There wouldn't been any moralizing on their part. The moment they got him in their sights, he was as good as dead. The thought did not settle well with Jack Grimaldi. He had lived for too long to end his days dead and forgotten in a godforsaken jungle somewhere in the wilds of Guàtemala. The powerful urge to live rose in him, and he was determined not to fall into the hands of the Communist rebels.

A slight sound off to his left made Grimaldi turn. He had a blurred glimpse of one of the guerrillas edging through the foliage. The man's line of travel would bring him close to Grimaldi, and the pilot decided it was time to initiate the action.

The AK-47 rose smoothly to Grimaldi's shoulder. He leveled the muzzle, tracking the stalking guerrilla for a few more seconds before he eased back on the trigger. The AK-47 rapped out its burst with a loud crackle of noise. Screeching birds erupted from the undergrowth. Startled monkeys, high in the trees, voiced their disapproval. Shell casings glittered as they were ejected from the Kalashnikov. And the guerrilla was slapped off his feet by the stunning impact of the 7.62 mm bullets.

The moment he had fired, Grimaldi altered his position, dropping low to scuttle through the undergrowth. He had gone barely six yards when the AK-47 belonging to one of the guerrillas opened up. The rebel held the trigger back and raked the foliage around Grimaldi with a continuous burst of autofire. Leaves were shredded and wood chips filled the air as the stream of slugs howled over Grimaldi's head. The firing ceased abruptly as the Kalashnikov exhausted itself.

The third guerrilla, on Grimaldi's right, began to yell to his companion. They conversed for several seconds as they attempted to coordinate their efforts.

In the meantime Grimaldi had traveled swiftly through the dense undergrowth, swinging around the edge of the clearing. He suddenly rose to his feet, the Kalashnikov snapping to his shoulder. He found his target and touched the trigger. The AK-47, back on semiauto mode, spit out a 7.62 slug that crashed through the target's skull and erupted from the far side. The Guatemalan terrorist uttered a brief cry before the impact of the slug silenced him for eternity. He lurched off balance and plunged headfirst into the pool. As his body floated to the surface, facedown, a billow of scarlet began to spread out from under him.

Before Grimaldi could move again, the remaining rebel opened fire. He was on the far side of the pool now, his weapon—an Uzi—ripping out its sound as it fed 9 mm slugs into the chamber at a cyclic rate of 600 rpm.

Grimaldi felt a couple of the slugs graze the sleeve of his shirt. He heeded the warning and dropped out of sight long enough to bring the Kalashnikov on target. He poked the muzzle through the undergrowth and triggered off a couple of shots in the direction of the Guatemalan terrorist. His second shot came close enough to throw the guy off his stride. The Uzi stopped firing. Grimaldi returned to autofire. He picked up his target as the Guatemalan dodged around the perimeter of the pool, tracking the man, and stroked the trigger. The Kalashnikov spit out a lance of flame. Grimaldi countered the natural rise of the muzzle, holding the weapon on line. He was rewarded by the sight of the guerrilla's shirt being blown to tatters, followed by a mist of red as the 7.62 mm slugs chewed through flesh and into vital organs. The rebel went down with a long scream rattling from his throat. As he crashed to the ground, kicking up decaying leaves, his Uzi flew from his fingers and dropped into the pool with a soft splash.

Grimaldi broke cover and moved quickly to where the first guerrilla lay. He relieved the man of his extra AK-47 magazines. The guy had also been carrying a 9 mm Browning Hi-Power. Grimaldi took it, along with the extra magazines he found in the guy's backpack. There wasn't much else useful to his survival. Grimaldi found a supply of drinking water, for which he was grateful, but couldn't find any food. He shrugged off the disappointment. He had survived so far, and waiting a little longer couldn't possibly hurt him. The Guatemalan was also carrying a sharp-bladed machete; the broad knife would come in handy for hacking away the tangled undergrowth that often hindered travel through the jungle. Grimaldi loosened the belt that supported the sheath in which the machete was kept. He strapped the belt around his own waist, grabbed the dead rebel's water bottle and moved on. He wanted to be well away from the area just in case more of the rebels turned up.

He checked his position and headed back into the jungle, feeling a little more secure once he had the enclosing forest all around him.

Now all he had to do was find Dragon Slayer and take it away from the Spetsnaz who had been left to guard it.

12

"We are looking for some friends," Katz began. "Our friends are likely to be in the hands of a group of FAR Marxist guerrillas. The group operates in this general area, and information we have received tells us that you have dealt with them and obtained supplies for them from time to time."

Jorge's sweating, bloody face assumed an expression of hurt innocence. Clearly he was weighing what to say next, and he darted quick glances at Katz and McCarter, who was standing next to the window.

"Before you make any denial," Katz warned, "remember how fragile your position is. We will not hesitate to use any methods to get the information we need."

"Let us say I did have contact with these Communists," Jorge said. "I myself am not a Communist, you understand. I believe in a man having freedom of choice."

"As long as that choice allows him to do business with anyone he wants," McCarter said. "Including terrorists."

"Business is business," Jorge stated fiercely. "If a man comes to me with a deal, I do not ask him what his politics are."

"That's bloody liberal of you," the Cockney remarked.

"I assume this business contact of yours has a base?" Katz asked. "Somewhere isolated where he's not liable to be disturbed."

Jorge shrugged. "Maybe."

Katz banged his prosthesis down hard on the table. "I don't want 'maybe' or 'perhaps.' Give me a straight answer, Jorge, or my restless friend by the window will have to give your memory a jolt."

The bandit eyed McCarter's tall figure. Then he appeared to reach a decision. "Do you have a pen?" he asked. "Paper?"

Katz fished a ball-point pen from his pocket. He laid it on the table. In the meantime McCarter located a sheet of creased paper on the floor and passed it across.

Jorge took the items and bent over the paper. It took him a few minutes to mark out a crude map. He looked at it to satisfy himself that he had it right, then he returned pen and paper to Katz.

"We are here," Jorge explained, indicating with a grubby finger. "You must travel along this line. North and a little east. Here you will come to hilly country. At the base of the hills there are many ravines and canyons. You will find a narrow river here. Where it bends near the mouth of this canyon, you will find the entrance to the base. It lies deep inside the canyon."

"Who is in charge of this group?" Katz demanded.

"His name is Salazar," Jorge said. "A very violent man. *Señor*, I can tell you no more."

"Only one thing," Katz said. "Is Salazar entertaining some foreign visitors at present?"

Jorge held up a hand. "*Señor*, do you really wish to see me dead? If not, please do not ask me such a question. I cannot answer."

Katz smiled. "You just gave me the answer I need."

An expression of admiration shone in Jorge's feral eyes. "You are a clever man, *señor*. Would that I had your mind. Then I could get out of this accursed jungle."

"Bloody hell," McCarter said sarcastically. "He'll be giving you flowers and a box of chocolates next."

Katz moved from the table and crossed to where James was still bending over Rios. The black commando glanced up at Katz, shaking his head slowly.

Just then Encizo came through the door and joined the Phoenix commander. "I've checked all the rooms. Made sure there are no open doors." He motioned to Katz. "Those boxes we passed on the way in. They contain Soviet-made weapons and explosives. I'm glad I hadn't known that when that hombre fired a shotgun in my direction and the buckshot slammed into those crates. That was scary enough without knowing they could have blown up. Actually it's mostly plastic explosives. Pretty stable stuff. Similar to RDX compounds like C-4. Detonators, primacord, blasting caps and electric squibs were packed in other boxes. Everything you need to blow the hell out of just about any target smaller than Tallahassee."

"I'm sure Jorge won't mind if we help ourselves to some of these items," Katz remarked. "Especially since he isn't a Communist and doesn't really like dealing with them."

"It wouldn't hurt for us to have a bigger stock of explosives," McCarter agreed. "Even if our demolitions expert isn't with us yet."

"Hopefully we'll be able to give him a present of some of these supplies when we find him," Katz said in a soft voice. He did not want to think of the possibility of never finding Manning or finding him dead.

"The weapons are old-model AK-47 assault rifles and PPS submachine guns," Encizo continued. "Soviet surplus. None of the newer AKMs or AK-74 rifles. The sort of stuff the USSR supplies to Third World countries and so-called revolutionaries."

McCarter looked at Jorge and grinned. "And you were just holding these crates for a friend?" he inquired. "No idea what was in them, eh?"

"I'm not a curious man," Jorge replied. "And I respect my clients' privacy and property."

"Yeah," Encizo muttered. "I bet you're just loaded with principles."

Calvin James cursed as he knelt beside the still body of José Rios. The black commando had covered the CIA agent with a blanket to keep him warm as part of a treatment for shock. He now pulled the blanket over Rios's face.

"He's gone," James announced as he stood. The hardass from Chicago glared at Jorge. "You useless ass—"

James stopped in midsentence and stormed out of the room. Jorge glanced at the faces of the other three Phoenix warriors. Their expressions made him tremble. "You promised you would not kill me," the bandit insisted.

"I'm not sure we should keep our word to scum like you," McCarter hissed.

"Maybe we should lock Jorge out of sight until we leave," Encizo suggested. "Let me check some of the smaller huts at the edge of the village and decide which one would be the best holding cell. I noticed one has bars in the windows."

"Take him," Katz replied. "I don't even want to see his murderous face again."

"No," the Cuban insisted. "Let me make sure the hut is secure first. You can put up with him for about fifteen minutes."

Katz nodded. He wondered what Encizo had in mind.

"What do we do with the Commie arsenal?" McCarter inquired as he watched Encizo leave the room.

"Blow it up," Katz answered. "Make sure it never winds up in the hands of the FAR or any other gang of lowlifes. You can go get the truck, David. The rest of us will take care of Jorge and the weapons in the arms room."

"I don't suppose we could have a little trial here, find Jorge guilty of murder and execute him?" McCarter inquired.

The bandit's face seemed to drain of color.

"Lucky for you we don't do things that way," Katz told Jorge.

"I guess you're right," McCarter muttered. "We didn't pack our kangaroo suits to have the court done that way."

THE REST OF THE BANDITS were herded together into one of the more solid buildings. Given time, there was no question they could break out of there. And when they did, they could deal with their dead comrades, who were left laid out in one of the adobe dwellings. Phoenix Force would not deal with them, and besides, they had their own unfinished business to attend to.

José Rios was buried in an unmarked grave outside the tiny hamlet. Katz guarded Jorge as he demanded that the bandit dig the grave for the man he had murdered. When the hole was ready, James and McCarter lowered Rios's corpse into the ground, wrapped in the blanket as an improvised shroud. They didn't want Jorge to touch the agent's body.

"You were a good man, José," James said at the graveside. "You deserved better than to wind up here with an unmarked grave. We'll make sure your father in East L.A. is taken care of and that he knows his son died a hero, even if he can never know the exact events that cost you your life."

"Amen," Katz said solemnly.

They shoveled the earth into the grave and buried Rios. As they were finishing the grim chore, Encizo approached and pointed his H&K subgun at Jorge.

"I'm going to lock you in the hut now," the Cuban announced. "I'll nail the door shut. You'll have a knife inside the hut—the same one you used to kill Rios with. You can use it to pry the bars out of one of the windows. That adobe will give way after a couple hours of hard work. But mark my words—don't break down the door. You won't know for sure if one of us stayed behind to watch you. Come out through the

door, and we'll figure you're going to try to warn the
FAR and their Russian pals. Come through the door,
and you might pay for it with your life. *¿Com-
prende?*"

"*Sí,*" Jorge confirmed with a weary nod.

"Move it," Encizo said, and ushered the bandit
across the village to the hut he had chosen for a cell.

"What the hell is Rafael up to?" McCarter wondered out loud. "What's all that business about those
conditions that Jorge has to agree to while he's in that
hut?"

"I suppose we'll find out," Katz answered. "Is the
truck ready?"

"Yeah," the Briton replied. "Got our spare gear
and the explosives we want to take. Charges are set in
the room with the Soviet weaponry. The timer is set for
five minutes. That will give us plenty of time to get
clear of this place."

"You didn't switch it on, did you?" James asked.

"Give me a little credit," McCarter snorted. "I'll
turn it on just before we leave."

"You can do it now," Encizo announced as he
walked toward his teammates. "Jorge is locked in his
cell, and I nailed the door shut."

"Shit," James groaned. "That sucker will kick the
door open as soon as he hears us leave. He isn't gonna
buy that crap that we 'might' have somebody watching the door. I just hope he doesn't manage to reach
the arms room to disconnect the charge."

"He won't," Encizo assured his teammates. "Come
on. We've been here long enough."

JORGE CRANED HIS NECK to peer through the bars to the window. He saw the four men climb into the truck and heard the engine start. Jorge sneered as he watched the vehicle drive from the village. The sound of the truck grew more faint as the Phoenix commandos drove farther away from the site.

"*Cachorros,*" he muttered with disgust.

Those *yanqui* bastards must have considered him to be a fool. He knew they hadn't left anyone behind to see whether he would leave the hut by the door or spend long hours digging at the bars with the knife. Jorge was not about to work at the bars to loosen them from adobe when he could easily kick the door open and hurry to the main building to disconnect the charge before it could blow the valuable arms to hell. Why should he let such profitable merchandise be destroyed?

Jorge slammed a boot into the door. It swung open from the kick. The bandit boss heard a loud snap and glanced down to see the rattrap nailed to the door frame. When he kicked the door open, it tagged the pedal tip with a nail to spring the trap. He frowned when he noticed a length of string tied to the steel bow of the trap. The string extended to the corner of the hut. Jorge's eyes trailed the string to a small metal sphere held in place by electrical tape.

"*¡Madre de Dios!*" Jorge exclaimed when he realized the object was a grenade.

The pin lay on the ground, the string tied to the ring. The Cuban had rigged the booby trap to spring the rattrap when the door opened, and the string was tugged to pull the loosened pin from the grenade by the action of the trap snapping shut. Jorge reached for the grenade in a desperate effort to yank it from the wall and hurl it into the jungle before it went off.

The grenade exploded in his face.

PHOENIX FORCE HEARD THE BLAST as they drove through the jungle. McCarter stopped the truck and glanced at his watch. The five minutes hadn't passed, and the sound of the explosion wasn't loud enough to be the charge set at the enemy arsenal. Rafael Encizo uttered an exaggerated sigh.

"I told him not to use the door," the Cuban commented with a shrug.

"That was sneaky, Rafael," James declared. "A real dirty trick."

"I thought you'd like it," Encizo replied in a flat voice. "Jorge made the decision to go through that door just as he decided to stick a knife in Rios. I even told him if he didn't use the window it could cost him his life. He didn't listen."

"It can be dangerous not to heed warnings," Katz agreed.

They waited until they heard the second explosion, which signaled the destruction of the Soviet weapons in the village. Satisfied, Phoenix Force continued to move through the Guatemalan rain forest, heading for the Spetsnaz base.

13

Grimaldi's keen sense of direction, plus all his years as a flyer, made him an excellent navigator. It made little difference whether he was in the air or on the ground. The Stony Man pilot was never truly lost for very long. By late morning he knew he was close to where the Russians and their Guatemalan partners had walked in on the Phoenix rescue mission.

He pushed on through the sweltering jungle mass, pausing every now and then to confirm his position. Checking and double-checking, he watched the sky whenever he could to read the position of the sun. Grimaldi knew the signs to watch for in the wild to enable him to check his position a number of ways.

It was almost noon when he noticed that the wind had grown stronger. Grimaldi had been aware of increased air movement for some time, even in among the heavy forestation. The wind brought with it the smell of the ocean, indicating that it was coming in off the Pacific. It confirmed that Grimaldi was heading in the right direction, but also warned him that there was a possible weather change in the offing. As time passed the force of the wind increased until it was tugging at his clothing, and then Grimaldi felt the first drops of rain. Within minutes the rain was falling heavily, filtering through the foliage.

A full-blown storm was due. Grimaldi knew how they could build to extremes, forming out on the ocean and then sweeping inland to strike with relentless fury. Depending on its eventual strength, the storm might blow itself out quickly or rage for hours. Anything in its path could be swept aside.

Putting his head down, Grimaldi battled against the rising force of the wind, trying to ignore the driving rain as he moved on.

He took a break a quarter hour later, sheltered beneath the gnarled roots of a huge tree. Laying aside the AK-47, the Stony Man pilot unstrapped his watch and turned it over. He unscrewed the back plate to expose a digital face. Touching a tiny key, he activated the micro receiver built into the watch. The receiver was a new gadget developed by the research department responsible for Dragon Slayer. It was designed to pick up a signal sent out by Dragon Slayer within a two-mile radius. The signal, tuned to the micro receiver's frequency, was automatically sent out by the helicopter and was intended as an emergency backup for use in extreme circumstances. Grimaldi had decided that his situation could easily be classed as extreme.

Grimaldi studied the pulsing red light flashing on the small face of the receiver. It was weak, indicating that he was on the periphery of the signal. He touched another button and watched the single pulse change to a grid pattern. Inside the watch the receiver began a simplistic triangulation program, taking as its root the signal itself. Within the microunit commenced the process that would take the incoming signal, combine it with transmitted pulses of its own and then calculate the location of the source. It was basic mathematics but would hopefully provide Grimaldi with a location for Dragon Slayer within fixed parameters. The microunit was a purely experimental device, given to Grimaldi by the micro techs who had asked him to field-try it if the opportunity arose. The Stony Man pilot had figured his luck was still holding when he had been allowed to keep his watch after capture by the Russians.

The signal displays on the grid pattern established themselves, showing the source of the transmission and Grimaldi's own position. As he advanced in the direction of the source, Grimaldi's signal would monitor his progress. If he veered off the direct line, the microunit would indicate his loss of course and visible increase in the pulse signal would show until he regained his course.

Grimaldi returned the watch to his wrist, with the microunit uppermost. He emerged from his temporary cover and continued his trek through the drenching rain.

With one eye on his direction finder the Stony Man warrior closed in on the helicopter and its guards. Grimaldi accepted the fact that when he reached Dragon Slayer he was going to have a fight on his hands in order to repossess the machine. The prospect of combat didn't worry him. He'd been involved in his share over the years, and though he had never considered himself a hero, Grimaldi had never shirked his duty. When it came down to a fight in order to survive, he had always found the motivation. And this time there was more at stake than just his own life.

Back along the line there was Gary Manning and Ilya Roskov. Grimaldi hadn't forgotten them, nor was he prepared to abandon them.

Twice during the next half hour the microunit displayed its warning signal as Grimaldi drifted off course. He regained his path, pushing through dense undergrowth that seemed to have a life of its own. Supple vines clung to his legs, slowing his passage. Thorny bushes ripped his clothing and scratched his flesh. The earth underfoot turned swampy, engulfing his feet in a muddy morass. He learned not to rush, but to take his time. Fighting the jungle and the stormy elements was nothing but a waste of effort. The harder he pushed, the more he was resisted. The only way to make real progress was to keep moving forward at a plodding, steady pace. He had to ignore the sluicing rain and the rising wind that raced through the forest with ease.

He almost missed the moment when the microunit showed the meeting of the two light pulses. His signal had begun to merge with that of the source.

And that meant Dragon Slayer was very close.

Grimaldi moved with caution now, not wanting to walk into the cold gun muzzle of some alert Spetsnaz or his guerrilla partner.

He crouched and bit by bit eased himself into the dripping undergrowth ahead of him, pushing aside the branches. On the far side of the clearing that opened out before him was his goal.

Dragon Slayer.

From his place of concealment Grimaldi was able to see the combat helicopter clearly. He could also see the four Spetsnaz troops and the Guatemalan guerrillas.

They had rigged a lean-to out of their waterproof capes and some long canes cut from the foliage. They were squatting together under the cover, staring out at the rain tumbling from the gray sky. Wind snatched at the cover, threatening to drag it clear of the canes.

One of the Spetsnaz climbed to his feet and reluctantly stepped into the open. He began to plod wearily around the perimeter, taking his turn at sentry duty.

As he watched the Russian, an idea formed in Grimaldi's mind. It was sketchy, but the bare bones began to flesh out as the Stony Man flyer observed the route the Spetsnaz was taking.

Grimaldi melted back into the undergrowth, then began to circle around the edge of the clearing, keeping the Russian in sight all the time. He moved as quickly as he could under the circumstances, pushing his way through the sodden vegetation, hunching his shoulders against the driving rain and the gusting wind. The one good thing about the storm was that it drowned out any noise he might make.

Grimaldi's timing was perfect. He reached the extreme curve of the clearing's far end thirty seconds before the Russian. The pilot was able to study the Soviet as the guy approached. The Spetsnaz was not enjoying his tour of duty. He was wet and cold, buffeted by the high wind, and could have been in a better place. Rain had soaked his combat fatigues and ran in continuous streams down his stern face.

The Russian soldier moved under the relative cover of a dense, leafy canopy, and tucked his AK-47 under one arm, fishing in a pocket for a cigarette. He pulled out a crumpled pack, took one out and stuck it between his lips. Then he located a cheap tin lighter, flicking the wheel a number of times before it caught. Cupping both hands around the flame, the Soviet bent his head as he attempted to light the cigarette.

It was now or never, Grimaldi decided.

He rose from his hiding place, lunging into the open, the AK-47 in his hands rising and falling like a club. The hard wooden butt crashed against the side of the Russian's skull, driving him to his knees. Grimaldi didn't hold back. There was no time for hesitation. He struck again, before the badly dazed Russian could respond in any way. A soft grunt burst from the man's lips as the AK-47 drove home. He arched over onto his back, one hand snatching at the sodden ground in a dying reflex action before he became still.

Grimaldi put down his weapon and caught hold of the dead Russian's feet. He dragged the man into the undergrowth, then bent over the body. He spent the next couple of minutes stripping the combat fatigues from the Russian. He pulled the garments over his own clothing, finishing with the Spetsnaz trooper's belt and the beret. Picking up his Kalashnikov, Grimaldi stepped out of the undergrowth and began the return journey to the helicopter.

He was well aware that his actions could get him killed. At a distance, in the driving mist of heavy rain and with the wind tugging at his clothing, he might easily be mistaken for the Spetsnaz trooper. He knew, however, that once he got close to the spot where the others were waiting, his odds were going to change dramatically. If one of the other Spetsnaz troopers spoke to him in Russian, then the game would be over. Grimaldi did not speak or understand the language.

He knew that once he got close, he was going to have to take the opposition out hard and fast.

Grimaldi checked the AK-47, making certain that it was cocked and ready for firing. Despite the pouring rain his mouth felt very dry. Sweat beaded the insides of his hands.

He plodded steadily toward the helicopter.

One of the Guatemalan guerrillas looked in Grimaldi's direction. He made a remark, causing one of the Russians to glance over his shoulder at the advancing figure.

Grimaldi tensed, hoping that the Russian wasn't about to speak. But he did—yelling something into the wind. All the flyer could do was raise his hand in a gesture of acknowledgement.

The Russian threw a hard glance at his companions.

Yet another challenge came Grimaldi's way, and he knew this time that the game was over.

"Goddamn it to hell!" the Stony Man pilot exclaimed.

And then he took the fight to *them* at full tilt.

He went fast, breaking to the right, then stopping in his tracks, the AK-47 rapping out its hail of 7.62 mm projectiles.

One of the Spetsnaz went down, blood spewing from between his shoulders. He struck the rain-sodden ground in a twisted heap.

Grimaldi still had the edge and he held on to it, even as the group scattered, the Kalashnikov expending red-hot death.

Two of the guerrillas were caught in the deadly stream, holes appearing in their jerking bodies as the

ComBloc slugs ripped into them, tumbling them groundward.

Grimaldi had made it to Dragon Slayer's tail section. He ducked under the lower body, emerging on the far side, where he came face-to-face with one of the two remaining Russians.

The Spetsnaz snapped off a burst form the AK-47 he carried.

Grimaldi felt something burn a scalding track over his ribs on the right side. He twisted his body around to face the Russian, triggering a wedge of slugs from his own weapon. The Soviet commando was thrown off his feet when the bullets crashed into his chest. Blood darkened the combat fatigues as the Spetsnaz went down.

The remainder of the group had spread apart, still moving away from the helicopter, each man trying to gain some space.

Moving swiftly along the glistening length of Dragon Slayer, Grimaldi touched a square panel set in the fuselage close to the entrance hatch. The panel opened to expose an illuminated keypad. Grimaldi tapped in the access code. The hatch unsealed with a subdued hiss of hydraulics.

Grimaldi heaved himself inside, his fingers reaching out to activate switches and buttons. Dragon Slayer sprang to life around him. The hatch thumped tightly shut. Above his head the rotor blades began to rotate. The soft hum and click of electronics filled the cabin. Filtered air drifted silently from the conditioner.

Beyond the toughened Plexiglas screen the surviving Spetsnaz and the Guatemalan guerrillas regrouped, turning their attention back toward Dragon Slayer.

The menacing snout of the rotary cannon powered around to track the group as Grimaldi's fingers flicked across the fire control panel.

With apparent disregard for the cannon, the surviving Spetsnaz raised his AK-47 and unleashed a stream of 7.62 mm rounds at Dragon Slayer. A number of the bullets impacted against the screen, leaving dull indentations in the Plexiglas.

Grimaldi, well aware that the next shots might be aimed for the rotors, reacted instinctively. His finger touched the Fire button set in the control column.

The multibarreled cannon erupted with a shattering roar, blasting continuous streams of steel-jacketed slugs at the opposition. The group vanished in a maelstrom of lethal autofire that reduced them to bloody shreds.

Boosting the power, Grimaldi eased Dragon Slayer off the ground and into the air, taking the combat chopper high above the treetops.

Keying his throat microphone, the Phoenix pilot spoke to the waiting *Anaconda*. Seconds later the carrier's acknowledgment reached his earphones.

"Glad to hear from you, Dragon Slayer. What is your situation? Over."

"A hell of a ways from being satisfactory, Base One. I'm on my own. Two of our people are still in the opposition's hands. Am about to attempt to change that. You have any good news for me? Over."

"A rescue team was dropped on a local beach in the early hours of this morning," the *Anaconda* informed Grimaldi. "Four men. Code-named Phoenix.

Their instructions were to attempt to locate and free the three of you if they found you had been taken captive. Over."

"Thanks for some good news, Base One. I'll try and join up with them. If we pull our people out, I can ship them back. Barracuda isn't going anywhere for a while. There's evidence they used machetes down there to try to cut a clearing, but they sure don't have anything long enough to serve as a runway in the jungle. If the storm doesn't let up, the ground will be waterlogged, and nobody will be able to fly that fancy MiG out of there. Over."

"We may be able to lift it out with helicopters and cranes," the voice from the radio replied. "But we're already flirting with a political powder keg here. I don't want to discuss this on the radio, but you know what I mean. Over."

"Affirmative," Grimaldi stated. They had conducted unsanctioned operations on Guatemalan soil without any sort of authority, and there were at least a dozen corpses in the rain forest from the U.S./USSR confrontation on Central American territory. It had all the potential to be a major international incident.

Grimaldi knew Guatemala to be a member of the Organization of American States, the Inter-American Treaty of Reciprocal Assistance and probably some other international outfits he wasn't even aware of. Nearly all of Central and South America belonged to the OAS, IATRA or both. Some of those countries would eagerly support any suggestions by Guatemala to demand restitutions from the United States. Of course, this could also lead to stormy debates in the United Nations. Uncle Sam had plenty of adversaries in the UN that would jump at a chance to criticize the U.S. and encourage sanctions against America. The shit could really hit the fan, Grimaldi realized.

"If we can't get Barracuda, we may have to destroy her," the pilot said. "You have the coordinates on the MiG if it comes down to that. I'll keep in touch, but better sign off now. Over."

"Good hunting, Dragon Slayer. Over and out."

14

The storm that had been threatening manifested itself in the final minutes before midday.

Rising wind and initial rainfall increased in intensity over a relatively short period. The sky opened, and a drenching deluge fell to earth. Having built up its power during the time it had raged over the Pacific, the storm tore inland with relentless ferocity. In the wake of the downpour came a high wind. It hurled the rain across the forested land, bending trees and uprooting what it could.

David McCarter found he had to hang on to the wheel of the swaying panel truck in order to keep it on a straight course.

"Bloody hell," he shouted above the noise of the storm. "Last time I saw weather like this was on the front at Blackpool in midsummer."

"Blackpool?" James asked.

"What?" McCarter replied, then realized James most probably hadn't heard of the place. "Seaside resort in England," he explained. "All funfairs and candy stalls. Like Coney Island, but with English fish and chips."

"Sounds great," James said without much enthusiasm.

McCarter grinned. "I knew you'd like it."

Ahead of them broken limbs from a tree crashed down across the rutted trail. Muttering to himself, McCarter put his foot down and barreled the panel truck through the leafy blockage. The vehicle lurched and bumped its way over the hefty length of wood.

"This is not a battle tank," Encizo explained to the Briton.

McCarter grinned at the Cuban. "But it thinks it is," he remarked as he jerked the wheel hard over.

Encizo tapped the side of his head. *"Loco hombre,"* he said.

"But you like him anyway," James pointed out.

"Sure," Encizo answered. "But only because I'm a little bit crazy myself."

The truck creaked and rumbled its way along the rutted track, and only McCarter's skilled driving kept it on course. The Briton, an expert driver, hadn't experienced such conditions for a long time. The last drive he had undertaken in difficult driving conditions had been on a rally he had taken part in six months back. That had been in the rugged mountain country of Wales, during a spell of bad weather. That had been hard enough, but at least he had been driving a specially prepared rally car. It had been equipped with heavy-tread tires and above-standard suspension. The engine had been overhauled and tuned up, and McCarter and his navigator had been strapped in their seats. The daredevil Briton wondered what the rally officials would have said if he had driven up to the start line in a battered old panel truck.

"Hey, you guys," McCarter yelled. "Looks like we're coming to the end of the trail."

The Force stared through the rain-lashed windshield. Up ahead the narrow trail petered out, blocked by a solid wall of greenery. McCarter drove up to the blockage, then turned the truck and pulled it close in beneath some overhanging branches. He switched off the motor.

Katz took a look at his watch. "We've been on this trail for over an hour and a half," he said. "It has gained some time for us, if nothing else."

"It's also kept us dry," James observed.

They all listened to the rain pelting against the roof of the truck.

"It's here to stay," McCarter commented. "Hey, how about if I stay behind and keep the motor running? Be ready for a quick getaway when you come back."

"As much as we'd like to take you up on that," Katz said, "I think we can make better use of your hidden talents."

McCarter looked grieved. "If you're sure."

"Who are you kidding?" Encizo asked. "David McCarter asking to stay out of a possible firefight?"

Picking up his KG-99, McCarter shoved open his door. "You know me, Rafael. I couldn't just sit back and let you fellers walk into trouble without being around to bail you out."

"The way he explains it almost makes it sound true," James observed.

Before they left the vehicle, the Force carried out a final weapons check, making sure that SMGs and handguns were fully loaded and that the grenades they carried were firmly in place. Knives and other pieces of equipment were secured.

Katz had been studying the crude map given to him by Jorge. He stared out through the windshield, looking over the tops of the trees ahead of them. Through the rain he could make out the ragged outline of a low range of hills. He pointed them out to the others.

"That's the way we go," he said.

Minutes later they were strung out in a line, tramping through the sodden forest. The heavy rain, pushed by the wind, beat its way through the dense foliage. To the men of Phoenix Force it was like marching beneath a never-ending shower. The water simply sluiced down from the canopy overhead. The spongy earth soaked up a great deal, but it wasn't long before the overwhelming volume of water became too much. Pools began to form, slowing the Force's progress.

Despite the conditions they didn't let up the pace, driven by the time factor that dominated their thoughts. They never lost sight of the fact that the lives of their partners might be hanging in the balance. Their mission was a search-and-rescue operation. The overriding priority was to get to their people and pull them out of Guatemala before something drastic happened.

The fate of the downed Russian jet was a lesser consideration. If time and circumstance allowed, they would also try to get the plane out.

Phoenix Force had to locate Manning, Grimaldi and Roskov and bring them back into the fold. They were operating on pure speculation at the present moment in assuming that their people were in the hands of the Russian advisers. All they really had to go on was Manning's last radio message, and they were working on the premise that the Soviets would want Ilya Roskov back alive—for a return to Moscow—and the kudos for the capture of a pair of American penetration specialists.

As far as Yakov Katzenelenbogen was concerned, it was the only line they could take. He put himself into the mind of the Spetsnaz commander, who had probably been told to locate the plane and its pilot. Russian tracking could have pinpointed the jet's landing place just as easily as had the U.S. Navy. After that it would have been a race against time as Soviet and U.S. groups searched for the plane and pilot. Although Manning and Grimaldi had reached home base first, the Russians had not been far behind. The Spetsnaz commander would have considered himself a fortunate man to locate the stolen jet and pilot and also to find the Americans involved, as well.

The next step would be to have Roskov taken off Guatemalan soil so he could be sent home. The same fate might be the lot of Manning and Grimaldi. It wasn't every day that American specialists fell into Russian hands. The knowledge they held inside their heads could prove invaluable to the Russian security community. Common sense would suggest having the Americans shipped to Soviet soil, where they could be worked on in secure surroundings and at a pace that would suit the methods of the KGB.

The removal of the three captives might prove to be a stumbling block. As the Russians were on Guatemalan soil in a totally unofficial capacity, they would be operating low-profile. They would not have instant access to transport of the type required to move three people out of the country at a moment's notice.

The needed arrangements indicated that a time of waiting could be expected. Katz guessed that the movement of the captives would be by sea. Possibly by submarine, maybe by surface vessel. It would all depend on what the Soviets had in the immediate vicinity and how soon it could arrive at a rendezvous point. The current storm might delay such an arrangement—which was good news for Phoenix Force—even though it might prove temporary.

But the unfavorable weather hampered Phoenix Force, too. A half hour of slow travel brought them to the foothills of the range described by Jorge's map. Following the undulating, thickly treed hills, the Force moved into the area crisscrossed with countless ravines and canyons. It was a difficult section to traverse, due to the fact that many of the minor ravines were hard to see under the spread of foliage. A number of the ravines were also watercourses, taking the overflow from the hills. The heavy storm had filled the courses with fast-running water, and there was much debris caught in the flow. Broken branches of trees, whole bushes. Each time the Force came across one of these churning streams, they had to divert from their path until a way could be found around the obstruction.

Rafael Encizo, moving slightly ahead of the others, came across the river. In normal circumstances this may only have been a shallow watercourse. With the overflow of water from the storm it had become a boiling torrent, spilling its banks.

Returning to the others, Encizo directed them to the river, where Katz called a brief halt.

"Luckily we're on the right side," the Israeli shouted above the rush of water and the high wind. "If we had been on the other side, I don't think we would have made it across."

The Phoenix Force commander pointed upstream. "We follow the natural course of the river," he said. "When we find the bend, we should be close to the canyon entrance. Keep your eyes open from here. The guerrillas may have posted an advance guard at the canyon entrance."

15

Kirov slammed the handset down and turned away from the radio. He strode out of the shack and stood on the steps, staring up into the dark sky, ignoring the lash of the falling rain.

"Is there a problem?" Lieutenant Litinov asked. The young officer was Kirov's second-in-command.

"The pickup will be delayed," Kirov snapped. "This storm is causing problems. It is going to slow the arrival of the ship."

"So we will have to entertain our guests for a little longer."

"It could well be more than just a little longer," the Spetsnaz commander explained. "No one seems to know just how long the storm may last. Damn! I could have done without this extra burden. We need all the time we can get to complete our main assignment."

"What are your orders, sir?" Litinov asked.

"Strengthen the guard. I can't explain why, but I'm getting the distinct feeling that we may be having visitors."

"Very well, Captain."

Kirov made his way across to the hut where the American specialist was being held. He nodded to the Spetsnaz on guard and entered, closing the door behind himself. Kirov shook the rain from his fatigues as he crossed the room.

The prisoner sat in a slumped position in his seat. His head was sagging forward against his chest. The front of the man's shirt was streaked with dried blood.

"Does your tongue feel looser now?" Kirov asked.

Gary Manning raised his head to stare at the Russian.

"No way," he said through heavy lips, each word making him wince. "I've nothing to say. We've been through this before," he added wearily. "You forget I know the game."

"Ah, but you may be interested to hear that due to unforeseen circumstances we now have more time at our disposal," Kirov said. "Not much comfort, but I'm sure that Karamatsov will find ways of making it entertaining for you."

When Manning didn't respond, Kirov scowled.

"Why do you insist on this refusal to cooperate? You will only succeed in making matters worse for yourself."

"That's what democracy is all about," Manning replied. "Being able to make a free choice in what you want to do."

"We will see how amusing you can be after Karamatsov has finished with you," he said, and strode from the hut, banging the door behind him.

When the door opened again, some five minutes later, Manning recognized the muscular form of Karamatsov. The Spetsnaz interrogator peeled of his cape, then crossed the room to stand in front of Manning. He smiled down at the helpless Canadian as he opened and closed his powerful fists.

Karamatsov's first barrage of blows was directed to the torso. Hard, telling blows delivered with precision and accuracy. Pain rushed through Manning's body. Each breath became an effort, wrenching sharp stabs of knifelike agony stabbing in and around his ribs.

After a time Karamatsov stepped back, studying Manning closely. Sweat beaded the Russian's taut brown face. "Talk now?" Karamatsov asked in his halting English.

Manning raised his head and stared at the man. "Go to hell," he said.

Karamatsov may not have had much of a grasp of English, but he understood Manning's reply. The Soviet shook his head, muttering to himself in Russian. Then he launched a full powered punch at Manning's jaw. It connected with a solid crack.

The blow rocked his head as blinding flashes of light flared before his eyes, and the room started to spin wildly. He felt everything begin to slip, as if the floor had tilted. Then the sensation ceased with jarring suddenness. The Canadian realized that he hadn't imagined the sensation. He was on the floor—the seat having tipped over, taking Manning with it.

Somewhere in the distance he could hear Karamatsov moving about. The Russian approached, took hold of the seat and pulled it upright.

Manning feigned unconsciousness, trying to clear his head. Peering through slitted eyes, he saw the room drift into focus. He watched Karamatsov pull on his cape and open the door. The man stepped outside, and the door shut.

The Phoenix warrior concentrated on regaining control of his faculties. Gradually he felt his equilibrium return. His breathing settled to a steady rhythm again.

Becoming aware then of a slackness in the rope binding his right wrist to the arm of the seat, he tested the rope again, flexing his arm and twisting his powerful wrist. He felt a slight give, and the wooden arm of the seat creaked a little. Manning realized that the fall had weakened the structure.

The glimmer of hope gave him renewed strength. He focused his strength in one direction—on his tethered right wrist. The muscles bulged beneath Manning's flesh as he worked tirelessly. Flexing, twisting, pulling.

With a sharp crack the wooden arm splintered, breaking away from the main frame of the seat. Manning wrenched his wrist free of the coiled rope. He opened and closed his fingers, encouraging the circulation to fully return.

Aware that Karamatsov or Kirov might return at any moment, Manning lost little time and continued to work on the rope securing his other wrist. With a gasp of triumph he drew his arm clear of the loosened rope. Leaning forward, he started the task of loosening his tethered ankles.

Finally he stood upright and stretched to relax his stiff joints before he made for the door.

He was just reaching for the handle when the door rattled, then began to open.

Swiftly Manning stepped to the side and positioned himself behind the door as it swung open.

Coming through the door was the armed guard who had been stationed outside. He was soaking wet from standing in the pouring rain. As he entered, he half turned to swing the door shut behind him. His eyes met those of Gary Manning. For a split second the guard simply stared. The eye contact was brief, but was maintained long enough to lose the guard any advantage he may have had.

Manning did not allow the time to go to waste. He jammed his left shoulder against the door, pushing it shut. At the same time his right fist struck with deadly force. It crunched against the guard's jaw, the impact releasing a great deal of concentrated energy. The Russian's head snapped back, his eyes glazing over. His legs buckled, and he sank toward the floor. Manning struck hard at the back of the Soviet's exposed neck. When the blow landed, the guard flopped limply, his arms and legs splayed wide.

Manning bent over and took the unconscious man's belt, which held pouches containing magazines for the AK-47 the Russian had been carrying. Buckling the belt around his waist, Manning snatched up the AK-47, then checked that it was loaded and cocked, ready for use.

He was armed and relatively free.

But where did he go from there?

16

The storm raging around the Soviet carrier *Chekov* matched Major Yuri Tchenko's black mood. The KGB man felt frustrated at the way events were taking place beyond his control. At first everything had seemed simple. Barishnov, on board the *Pushkin*, had not only tracked the Barracuda but had also pinpointed its landing place in Guatemala. He had then contacted a Soviet Spetsnaz unit operating undercover with a local guerrilla group, and had assigned them the task of detaining the defecting pilot and securing the downed plane. This had gone ahead and had seemed to be running smoothly. Then the Spetsnaz had come up against a team of American specialists obviously sent in to assist Roskov. There had been a firefight, due to the inability of the local guerrilla commander to control his men. The Americans had been captured alive, along with Roskov. On the return march to the guerrilla base one of the captured Americans had been lost in a fall from a high ridge. And then, to add further difficulties, a severe storm had blown up. It was delaying the removal of Roskov and the surviving American from Guatemalan soil and was also hampering the salvage operation designed to recover the Barracuda.

Tchenko's helplessness had been compounded only minutes earlier when he had received a radio call from the *Pushkin*. His contact, Barishnov, had reported the transmission between an unidentified American vessel and a man who appeared to be the missing American. There had been talk of an attempt to salvage Barracuda as well as a rescue of the other American and Roskov. It had also been learned that more of their specialists had landed on Guatemalan soil.

The moment he had digested the implications of the message, Tchenko got back to Barishnov with instructions to update Kirov immediately. The Spetsnaz commander was ordered to maintain security at the base until the retrieval squad arrived to take charge of Ilya Roskov and the American. He was also alerted to the likelihood of an attack from the American specialist team on the ground, as well as from the American who had escaped.

Tchenko had returned to his cabin, his mind full of conflicting thoughts and emotions. There was so much at stake, he realized. Not least was the possibility of the Americans getting their hands on a Soviet fighter plane of advanced design. There was also the chance of losing the defecting pilot to the Americans. Tchenko was aware that Roskov was in Soviet hands. He would not, however, feel totally secure until the traitor was out of Guatemala. Tchenko could not allow himself to become complacent. Too many things could happen to change the order of the day. He had learned over the years that it was never a wise thing to take too much for granted.

There was also the Spetsnaz operation to consider. A great deal of time and effort had been expended on behalf of the ailing Guatemalan rebels. The overall number of Communist subversives in Guatemala had been substantially reduced over the previous few years. Despite the harsh treatment meted out by the military, the guerrillas maintained a hit-and-run policy. They would strike at a target, then melt back into the jungle where they could easily hide in the trackless expanses. Instability in the Guatemalan government structure also aided the guerrillas, as it filtered down to the military. Aid for the guerrillas, in the form of Soviet weapons, came in from El Salvador, Honduras and even Mexico. But weapons were not always the answer. It had been decided that the Guatemalan Communists needed a boost to their morale. That was why the strike at the country's largest oil field was planned, destroying oil rig and storage facilities. The act was meant to embarrass the government, lose the administration sorely needed funds from the sale of the oil, and would also show the nation that the FAR was still a force to be reckoned with. The decision to send in a Spetsnaz unit had come directly from the KGB hierarchy in Moscow. They wanted the FAR strike to be successful and had decided to make a definite contribution to the initial planning of the operation. Once the guerrillas were trained and organized, the Spetsnaz intended to withdraw, leaving the final phase to the Guatemalans themselves.

But the scenario had changed drastically. The unexpected sequence of events had forced the Russian advisers to assume an active role, which increased the risk that their presence in Guatemala would become public knowledge. Such a revelation would do a great deal to harm Soviet credibility on the general global scene. As far as Tchenko was concerned, the new era of world peace allowed attention to be diverted from the covert agencies. They were able to push ahead with more long-term plans and operations. The world revolution would still take place, albeit at a slower pace and by slightly altered means.

But argument still raged within the Soviet power structure on the subject of the recent changes. Many of the old guard were opposed strongly to the changes, as were those bureaucrats who had something to lose. Internal wrangling and political maneuvering went on ceaselessly. Yet within the structure the KGB maintained a strong grip on Soviet activities in the global arena. The many tentacles of the powerful machine still lurked in the shadows, reaching out to manipulate, to gently nudge and push.

With all these thoughts in his mind, Yuri Tchenko brooded in the silence of his solitary cabin. He was aware of the responsibility that had fallen on his shoulders. Only one opportunity was going to present itself to rescue the whole affair to the credit of the Soviet Union. Once a course had been decided upon, there would be no turning back. Tchenko had no one to advise him. The situation required an on-the-spot decision, and as senior KGB man on the scene, that decision was up to him. He realized that if he pushed too hard, too far, the episode might escalate into something far more serious. On the other hand, there was no way his Kremlin masters would condone sitting back and doing nothing. The Americans were going to make the most of the situation. It was up to

Tchenko to face that threat. One way or another he had to make his choice.

The KGB agent left his cabin and made his way to the bridge, where he caught the eye of the carrier's captain. The bearded commander joined Tchenko, who drew him aside so that his words could not be overheard.

"We are faced with a delicate situation, Captain," the KGB man explained.

"I see," the captain replied. "Now that it's delicate, it becomes *our* situation."

"Levity is uncalled-for at the present time," Tchenko snapped.

"Excuse me, Major. You had better explain."

The captain listened in silence while Tchenko gave a detailed analysis of the situation. He did not utter a single word until the KGB man finished.

"What do you see as our options?" the captain asked.

"Either we maintain a discreet distance, observing but not participating, or we go to the aid of our comrades. There is also the matter of the Barracuda. The Americans, I am certain, will make an attempt to salvage the plane. They are not going to pass over the chance of getting their hands on one of our most advanced fighters."

The captain considered Tchenko's reply at length before speaking. "If we enter this game," he said carefully, "then we could find ourselves in a confrontation with the Americans."

"I have realized that possibility," Tchenko admitted.

"And if it becomes a reality?"

Tchenko turned slowly, his gaze unwavering as he faced the questioner. "Then we do whatever is necessary."

17

The entrance to the canyon yawned before them, obscured partly by piled-up boulders and a tangle of greenery.

Phoenix Force huddled in the thin cover provided by an overhang of mossy rock while they assessed the approach to the canyon.

"I don't see any easy way to do this," Calvin James said.

"One way in, one way out," Encizo stated, eyeing the formation of high rock escarpments into which the canyon cut.

"I'd be surprised if there are no guards some way in," Katz observed. "The problem is, we don't know how many. Or just where they are."

"One thing for sure," McCarter added. "We can't afford to sit around here for too long."

"What do you suggest, David?" asked James.

"We have to flush the beggars out," McCarter explained. "Get them to show themselves so we can take 'em out."

"How?" Encizo asked. "Whistle them up?"

"Not exactly," McCarter said. "It needs someone to walk in and let himself be seen. The rest stay out of sight and watch for movement. The minute a rebel pops his head up—*bang*!''

"Oh, great,'' James said with a sigh. "Real suicide stuff.''

"Look, it's a bloody sight better than sitting here doing bugger all. If it's getting shot at that's worrying you, I'll be your decoy. Just make sure you don't miss with that Yankee popgun, mate.''

Katz leaned forward. "Are you sure you want to do this, David?''

"Of course I don't *want* to do it,'' the Cockney admitted. "But we have to flush out any guns hidden up there.'' He grinned suddenly. "Oh, come on, you solemn beggars. Think I'd even suggest the idea without you guys to back me? Even this Chicago bum is worth ten of anybody else's best. Right, James?''

The black warrior smiled. "Right on, McCarter,'' he said.

"Good, let's get this circus on the road,'' the Briton declared.

"Hey, amigo,'' Encizo called as McCarter moved out. "Take it easy.''

"Caution is my middle name,'' McCarter replied.

As the Briton entered the canyon, stepping carefully over the tumbled rocks, Katz, James and Encizo filtered in behind him. They kept close to the rocky sides, pressing into the deep shadows that lay at the base of the craggy walls. Once within the confines of the deep canyon, they were shielded from the wind, though they could still hear it. Rain found its way down between the rock walls.

Ahead of Katz, James and Encizo, the tall figure of McCarter could be seen moving relentlessly forward.

He kept up a steady, unhurried pace, never once looking to left or right. The courageous Briton put all his trust in his three fellow warriors, letting them be his eyes for anything not directly ahead of him. McCarter would not have ventured such a scheme with anyone but his Phoenix teammates. They acted as one when they were together, each man looking out for the others during any action. They may have done it without conscious thought, but the feeling was there and it was mutual. The five Phoenix specialists had developed this unconscious bond through many perilous missions. In such a tightly bonded group as Phoenix Force, absolute trust in and dependency on each member was vital. Without it they would not have existed for so long. Nor would they have been so successful.

It was this bond that kept the Force going in their search for Gary Manning and Jack Grimaldi. None of them would relent until the missing pair were back in the fold.

The thought ran through McCarter's mind that there *was* another individual he would trust in such a situation as the one he was in right now.

That man was Mack Bolan.

David McCarter would have had no hesitation in placing his life in the capable hands of the man known as the Executioner. It had been Bolan, then in the guise of John Phoenix, who had been instrumental in helping to create the Stony Man project. He had been one of those involved in choosing the men who would make up Phoenix Force and Able Team. Bolan's inspiration had been the fire that had breathed life into the combat teams. The big guy, without ever having to say it, had made them all aware that he would never expect any of them to undertake a single mission he would not have accepted himself. If he expected them to put their lives on the line, it would be a line he would walk himself.

Such a leader drew the best from the people who worked with him. In fact he drew more than their best. When the chips were down, they excelled.

Well, Mack, I'm certain bloody sure to be putting that faith to the test right this minute, McCarter thought, as he made that long, lonely walk along the rain-drenched canyon floor.

The minutes dragged by with agonizing slowness. McCarter, wet and cold, heard nothing but the impact of the rain on the canyon floor. In the distance he could hear the drone of the wind. There was nothing else, not even the sound of his own footsteps. The sound of his own passing was drowned out.

McCarter hunched his shoulders against the cold fingers of rain sneaking down his back beneath his combat fatigues, wishing something, anything, would happen.

When it did happen, the suddenness jolted his nerves.

The flat crack of Calvin James's M-16 came abruptly. The sound racketed around the canyon, bouncing from wall to wall. In its wake came a second shot.

By then McCarter had thrown himself down, his body pressing close to the wet earth.

His mind was registering the second shot. That had come from Katz and his Uzi. No mistaking that sound.

Another sound reached McCarter's ears. It came from much closer than the shots. It was the rattle of disturbed stones trickling down the rocky lower slope of the canyon wall.

McCarter cursed to himself as he rolled over onto his left side, eyes raking the slope nearby.

And then he saw the dark-skinned Guatemalan rebel, half-running, half-sliding down the shale slope near the canyon floor, trying to keep his balance even while making an attempt to aim his Kalashnikov.

The Cockney warrior jerked his KG-99 into position as he pushed to his knees. Snap-aiming, he loosed off a burst that took away the rebel's choice of action. The 9 mm slugs pounding into his chest threw the rebel to one side. He lost control of his limbs and plunged facedown on the rocks, bouncing and twisting as he slithered to a halt.

McCarter climbed to his feet, rubbing his left knee where he'd banged it on his way down.

"David?" It was Katz's voice.

"Over here," the Briton called.

"You all right?" Katz inquired as he and the others rejoined McCarter.

"Probably got a few gray hairs," McCarter said. He glanced at James. "Took your bloody time with that shot, didn't you?"

The black commando maintained a straight face. "I knew you'd want to make the best of your performance, so I gave you all the time you needed."

"How did we do?" McCarter asked.

"Cal took the first one," Encizo said. "And Katz tagged the second."

"See," the Briton proclaimed. "I told you it was a brilliant idea."

"This one is still alive," Encizo called, bending over the rebel McCarter had brought down.

James took over and examined the wounded Guatemalan.

The rebel rattled something off in rapid-fire Spanish, too fast for Katz's limited command of the language. "What's he saying?" Katz asked.

"He says he doesn't want to die," James explained, "and wants us to help him."

"Let us bargain with him," Encizo said. He spoke to the rebel in Spanish. "My partner is a medic. He will tend your wounds in exchange for some information."

"Anything," the injured man promised.

"Were there just the three of you out here?"

"Yes."

"Are you holding prisoners at your base?"

"Yes. A Russian pilot and an American."

"Surely there were two Americans from the helicopter you saw?"

The rebel nodded. "This is correct. But one was lost during our return to the base."

"Lost?" James interrupted as he delved into his medical kit.

"He fell from a high ridge to the jungle below."

"Did he survive?" Encizo asked.

"We don't know. There wasn't time to look for him."

"What did he look like?"

The rebel gave a description that fitted Jack Grimaldi.

Encizo gave Katz and McCarter a translation of the conversation.

"Let's hope Jack made it," the Israeli said.

While James worked over the wounded man, Encizo asked him more questions.

"Gary is alive, by the sounds of it. So is Roskov. They have them in separate huts. It appears the Russians are stuck with them because they can't get any form of transport in until this storm blows over."

"Ask him why the Russians are in Guatemala," Katz suggested.

Encizo put the question to the rebel.

"He says the Russians came to help organize a major strike against the country's largest oil field. The idea is to destroy it as a show of strength on behalf of the Communist rebels. They want to indicate that they are not likely to go away—that the fight is far from over."

"Ivan up to his old tricks," McCarter said. "Doing his best to keep the pot boiling."

"But unofficially," Katz reminded the Briton. "I begin to see a KGB ploy here. The old guard refusing to knuckle under to Gorbachev's peace initiative. It's true what we've been hearing about behind-the-scenes wrangling. Gorbachev isn't having a completely smooth ride."

"It was bound to happen," Encizo said. "You don't change ideological policies overnight. And you don't get the hard-liners giving up without one hell of a fight."

Calvin James stood and crossed to stand with Katz and McCarter. "I've done what I can for him. He won't survive. Those bullets have caused a lot of internal damage. Nothing out here to help him.''

Katz glanced at the wounded rebel. The man appeared to be slipping into unconsciousness.

"I gave him an injection," James explained. "Told him it was a painkiller. Actually it will knock him out. He'll sleep away what's left of his life. Better than being in agony."

McCarter swore under his breath.

"It's a bloody world we live in," he observed, turning away and heading up the canyon.

The others followed, each man replenishing his weapon with a full magazine, ready for the battle that lay ahead.

18

Kirov emerged from the radio shack once again, having just been briefed. Things had certainly become a lot more complicated. The first question to enter Kirov's mind had to do with the escaped American. How had he regained control of his helicopter? The machine had been guarded by a number of Spetsnaz and guerrillas. The Russian did not allow the question to worry him too much. If the man had engaged the guards and disposed of them, then credit to him. It confirmed an old adage about never underestimating the enemy. Superiority had little to do with well-equipped forces or excellent training, in many cases. It often came down to simple things like a will to fight for what the enemy believed in with all his heart. For things like faith and determination and justice. Kirov, true Marxist that he was, had faced enough resistance in his military years to understand what drove men to extremes in battle. What gave them the will to win, even against overwhelming odds. He might not have subscribed to their beliefs, but he understood how they motivated people. He had come face-to-face with such beliefs in Afghanistan. There, in the bleak, rocky mountain wastes, the might of the Russian military machine had been unable to crush the resistance of the *mujahedeen*. Kirov had finished his tour of duty with great respect for the wiry Afghan fighters.

Crossing the rain-swept compound, his boots sinking into the soft mud, Kirov hunched his shoulders against the slap of the wind. Again his thoughts fixed on the immediate threat he was faced with. A force of American specialists in the area only added to his problems. Though they were not a sizable force, trained and well-equipped commandos were not to be easily dismissed.

Kirov entered the hut he was using as his command HQ. He closed the door behind him, knocking the rain from his fatigues. The hut comprised his sleeping area, with a table and a few hard chairs on the far side of the room.

The table had a large map spread across it. Lieutenant Litinov was bending over the map, discussing the proposed raid on the oil field with the guerrilla leader, Salazar. Litinov glanced up as Kirov entered, saw the expression on his commander's face and sensed at once that things were not going too well.

"Captain?"

Kirov stamped across the hut to where his AK-47 leaned against the wall. He stripped out the magazine and began to check the assault rifle.

Litinov left Salazar and joined the Spetsnaz commander.

"What is it, sir?"

The Russians had served together in Afghanistan. They had faced the *mujahedeen* and had camped out together on the bleak mountain passes. There were no secrets between them.

Kirov told his younger comrade about the radio message and what he deduced from it.

"You said we would regret this merger with the KGB," Litinov reminded him, drawing a taut smile from Kirov.

The Spetsnaz commander had not forgotten his remark. He had felt all along that the KGB was a strange bedfellow for the GRU, but circumstances often created unlikely liaisons.

In truth the Spetsnaz had little to do with the KGB. The elite fighting force came under the command of GRU, the Soviet military Intelligence agency. From time to time the KGB, mistrusted by most military departments, could exert its far-reaching influence and involve others in its schemes. That was why the Spetsnaz unit commanded by Kirov had found itself being transported to Guatemala to train Salazar's guerrillas. It hadn't been an assignment Kirov would have chosen for himself or his men, but it had been a direct order from his own superiors at GRU, so Kirov had kept his mouth shut and his eyes to the front. It had been lucky for him that the KGB had not yet perfected the trick of reading thoughts.

Reading between the lines, Kirov had sensed an alliance built on convenience. He was aware of disagreement with Gorbachev's new peace overtures. Many of the military hard-liners were feeling uneasy. They felt the softening of the stance toward the West would lead to erosion of the Soviet way. They preferred the tough approach, showing the enemy that there would be no backing down. The KGB, ever suspicious of anything liable to weaken its grip, had no intention of giving up the established patterns of power. As far as it was concerned, it was business as usual. To strengthen its hold, it forged ahead with covert schemes designed to push forward the grand plan of global Communism. The problem with the KGB was that it had existed for so long in a world of its own, full of plot and counterplot, deceit and treachery, that it saw no other way of doing things. Nor would it have wanted to change if anything had been suggested. The KGB lived and breathed in an atmosphere of noncompromise. It was Marxism right, left and center, with no allowance for deviation.

The Guatemalan scheme had been a classic KGB enterprise. A plot to upset the Guatemalan government by destroying one of its showcase industrial setups. In one decisive action the guerrillas would wipe out the oil field and also strengthen their own hand in the eyes of the people. The scenario followed the KGB training manual. Create confusion. Fear. Intimidation. Expose the enemy's weaknesses and promote the cause with determination.

The Guatemalan rebels, though enthusiastic, were by no means sophisticated. They lacked the finesse to carry through such an operation, and so it was decided to place a Spetsnaz unit under KGB command for the purpose of training and equipping the rebels.

Matters had come about that had changed the initial purpose of the Spetsnaz presence on Guatemalan soil, and now they seemed to be undergoing a further change.

"Do you think we're going to see some action?" Litinov asked.

"I'm not checking this weapon simply because I'm bored," Kirov replied.

He replaced the magazine and cocked the weapon. Then he took out his handgun and repeated the operation, returning the Makarov to his holster.

"Pass the word among the men," Kirov said. "Tell them to keep on their toes."

Salazar, who had been listening, left the map.

"What can I do, Captain?" he asked.

Kirov placed extra magazines in his pockets. "Those men of yours in the canyon. Are they dependable?"

"No one has ever got through before."

"I'm not talking about local traders," Kirov snapped. "The kind of men I mean would be highly trained penetration specialists."

"I trust my men," Salazar replied in an aggrieved tone.

"We will see," the Spetsnaz commander said, snatching up his AK-47 and following Litinov outside.

19

Gary Manning observed the sudden flurry of activity with interest. He had been estimating his chances of getting out of the hut and across the compound and had admitted them to be small. Despite the storm the compound was busy with armed men moving about. This activity increased after Captain Kirov had come out of the radio shack and crossed to a hut on the far side of the compound. When he had showed again, he had been accompanied by a young Spetsnaz officer and Salazar.

Orders had been passed, and men began organizing themselves around the compound. A machine gun was brought from one of the huts and set up behind an existing sandbag emplacement. A couple of the Spetsnaz soldiers were given an order from the captain that sent them away down the trail leading to the canyon entrance.

Manning had no way of knowing what had caused the general alert. It might be government troops. He even wondered about American rescue efforts for Barracuda and Roskov.

There was even the remote chance it might be Phoenix Force, though he knew he could be grasping at straws. On the other hand, he did not underestimate Stony Man resourcefulness. Hal Brognola, aided by his combat teams, had pulled off some pretty audacious tricks in the past. There was no reason not to expect them to do so again.

But until he had proof, Manning knew he was still going to have to rely on his own initiative. That meant getting himself out of the hut, freeing Roskov and clearing out of the area.

His train of thought was broken by the sight of the bulky Karamatsov heading across the compound—in the direction of Manning's hut. The Russian looked angry, his head twisting from side to side as if he was seeking someone.

And then Manning understood: Karamatsov had missed the Spetsnaz who was supposed to be on guard outside.

The Canadian gripped the AK-47, easing back from the door. His only chance was to take Karamatsov the moment he entered. It had to be done quickly and with a minimum of noise. Manning could not risk a shot.

The door crashed open as Karamatsov burst into the hut, his angry voice filling the emptiness. His keen eyes spotted the unconscious Spetsnaz on the floor, and he snatched for the Makarov holstered on his belt.

Manning kicked the door shut behind the Russian, jabbing the muzzle of the Kalashnikov into the small of his back.

"Hands on your head," he ordered sharply.

Karamatsov hesitated, his fingers curling around the pistol's butt.

"Do it," Manning snapped, cracking the barrel of the AK-47 against the Russian's knuckles.

Karamatsov swore. He had understood, though. His hands lifted, fingers spreading across his skull.

Reaching out, Manning took the Makarov and tucked it in his belt. He prodded Karamatsov across the hut. "Down on the floor," he ordered.

A scuffing sound from behind Manning distracted him briefly as the possibility of a rear-attack flashed into his mind. The Canadian's eyes flickered off Karamatsov for an instant. The noise must have reached the Russian, too, because he erupted into violent action, spinning on one foot, his other leg sweeping round in a scything motion. The circle-kick caught Manning's left hip, knocking him off balance.

Karamatsov followed through his initial move, launching himself at Manning with a growl of rage. His muscular body slammed into Manning, driving him across the room. Karamatsov clamped his thick fingers around the AK-47, preventing Manning from using it, and used his powerful legs to slam blow after blow to the Canadian's lower body and stomach. If Manning had been a man of lesser physique, he might have caved in under the relentless assault. As it was, he took the heavy blows while backpedaling in order to gain a few seconds.

Without warning Manning dropped to the floor, bringing up his right leg and planting his foot in Karamatsov's stomach. He employed the natural motion of both their bodies, lifting Karamatsov, then hurling him over his head. The Russian released his hold on the AK-47 as he was spun over Manning's body. He desperately tried to control his fall, but his timing was out and he crashed to the floor with a jarring thump.

By then Manning was on his feet and turning to face his opponent. The Phoenix warrior closed in as Karamatsov started to climb to his feet, shaking his head. As Karamatsov began to uncoil from the floor, Manning swung the wooden stock of the Kalashnikov in a sharp stroke that impacted against the Soviet's heavy jaw. The blow snapped Karamatsov's head around, and blood sprayed from the broken skin. The Spetsnaz stumbled back, still swinging his huge fists at Manning. The Canadian lashed out with the AK-47 a second time. The hard butt crunched directly between Karamatsov's eyes and the Russian toppled over, blood streaming from his nose. He moved sluggishly a few times and then lay still.

Manning turned to locate the source of the sound that had distracted him. The Spetsnaz guard was slowly regaining his feet, gazing around him with glazed eyes. He barely noticed Manning cross the room and never saw the AK-47 that cracked across the back of his skull, spreading him out on the floor again.

Locating a length of the rope that had previously bound him, Manning tied the Spetsnaz guard's hands behind his back. He took another length to repeat the operation, but when he checked Karamatsov, there was no sign of life. Manning tossed the rope aside and retrieved his assault rifle.

After he had stepped to the rear of the hut, Manning inspected the wall. He found a couple of loose timbers. He put his boot against the lower edge of the timbers and pushed, feeling them start to give. Manning spent the next few minutes moving the timbers back and forth until he had loosened them enough to create a gap. Kneeling, he peered through the gap. There was open space between the rear of the hut and the rocky slope forming the rim of the high basin in which the guerrilla base was located. Manning returned to the task of widening the gap in the timbers. The moment he had it large enough, he squirmed through, pushing the AK-47 ahead of him.

Once outside he was subjected to the extremes of the storm. Within a couple of minutes he was soaked to the skin. He ignored his discomfort, working his way along the rear of the huts until he reached the one where Ilya Roskov had been placed.

Manning knew that time was not on his side. His own escape might be discovered at any moment. Once that happened, his chance of freeing Roskov would lessen dramatically.

Edging along the side of the hut, thankful for the stacked crates and trash that offered cover, Manning reached the corner. He peered around it and saw a tall Spetsnaz guarding the door. Glancing out across the compound, the Canadian saw that there was still plenty of activity.

He decided that the only course open to him was direct action. In fact he had little choice in the matter. He took a deep breath, eased round the corner of the hut and strode up behind the Spetsnaz on guard. Manning rammed the AK-47's muzzle against the Russian's spine. The Russian stiffened. Manning prodded him with the assault rifle, then reached round to remove the guard's own weapon from his hand. Manning used his rifle to guide the man toward the door, pressing him against it.

"Inside," Manning ordered, forgetting that he was speaking to a Soviet soldier who did not necessarily understand English.

Using the muzzle of the confiscated AK-47, Manning tapped the door latch. The Spetsnaz trooper nodded. He reached down and unbolted the door, then pushed it open. He stumbled inside under pressure from Manning's rifle.

Ilya Roskov was sitting on a low cot, his back to the wall. He glanced up as the Spetsnaz appeared, not realizing immediately that the guard was minus his weapon.

"Let's go, Ilya," Manning said, showing himself as he closed the door.

Roskov stared at the Canadian for a moment. "How did you . . . ?" he began.

"We can discuss that later," Manning said.

He tossed the guard's AK-47 to Roskov as the pilot climbed off the cot. The guard was directed to the cot, where he was bound with his own belt. Roskov tore off a strip of blanket to gag him. The guard's spare magazines for the AK-47 were dropped into Roskov's flying-suit pockets, along with the Makarov pistol.

Back at the door Manning studied the scene outside. "Something's about to break," he explained to Roskov. "When it does, we make our break."

"This Captain Kirov will not give up without a fight," Roskov warned. "I have talked to him. He is a hard man. A good soldier."

"Do tell," Manning replied. "The same goes for me, Ilya Roskov. *I* don't quit and I'm a good soldier myself. Now, how about you?"

"Me? Oh, I am very good, too," Roskov said. "You will see."

"That's about the only thing we can be sure of," Manning said. "It's a fact that sooner or later we are going to be in the middle of a firefight."

20

The canyon ran on for a couple of miles. The sides rose sheer into the rain-streaked, gray sky, their tops green with trees. The floor of the canyon was strewn with broken, shattered rocks that ranged from fist-sized chunks to massive boulders as big as houses. Here and there patches of greenery relieved the monotony of drab stone.

Phoenix Force moved in single file along the canyon. For much of the time they were splashing through water that streamed along the bottom.

Calvin James took the point, scouting the way ahead, with Katz watching his back and also the left side of the canyon. Encizo came next, the right side of the canyon his area. McCarter brought up the tail. The ever-suspicious Briton made a good tail man.

They were nearing the end of the second mile when Calvin James made contact. The black commando broke into action at the same time he shouted a warning to his fellow warriors. "Spetsnaz. Ahead—two of them!"

James dropped to the ground, bringing his M-16 into the firing position.

Behind him the other Phoenix warriors reacted instinctively.

Katz dropped into a crouch, scanning his side of the canyon, then ahead, picking up the Spetsnaz pair, who were clad in camou fatigues.

With a quick twist of his body Encizo ducked behind a large chunk of rock edging the trail.

McCarter, professional to the last, checked the back trail, even though he was certain they had not been followed.

The confrontation lasted for scant seconds. Each party was aware of the consequences of any delay in reacting.

The well-trained Spetsnaz had their orders. If they came across any opposition, one of them was to return to the base to report while the other remained behind and did what he could to hold back the enemy.

They followed instructions exactly. One of them turned and headed back the way they had come, and the other began to lay down covering fire.

''Cal, the runner!'' Katz said sharply, understanding what the Spetsnaz were up to.

James had also recognized the Russians' strategy. He rose to one knee, bringing the M-16 to his shoulder and sighting in on the retreating figure of the Spetsnaz. Taking into account the poor visibility, James led his target, making allowance for the fact that he would be shooting over a range of at least 400 meters. James thumbed the selector switch of his M-16 from full auto to semi. The assault rifle had a maximum effective range of more than 500 meters, with greater accuracy in the semiauto mode. He aimed and squeezed the trigger. The moment he fired, the Spetsnaz trooper retaliated with an AK-47. However, the

Russian soldier's weapon was on full auto, and his 7.62 mm rounds missed the Phoenix pro.

"Shit," James rasped as bullets ricocheted against rock less than a yard from his position.

He aimed at the muzzle-flash of his opponent's Kalashnikov. The Spetsnaz gunman's head and shoulders were illuminated by the glare from his weapon. James squeezed off three shots, the M-16 still on semi. He saw his target jerk from the impact of at least one 5.56 mm slug. The AK-47 fell from the Russian's fingers as a massive jolt of pain, like a solid hammer blow to the chest cavity, sent the man into a wild convulsion. He crashed to the ground, his face slamming against hard rock.

Rafael Encizo saw the first Spetsnaz go down and broke cover to sprint across the area to where James lay in a prone position. The Cuban ran past the black commando and opened fire with his MP-5. The range was too great for the Heckler & Koch submachine gun, but Encizo intended to draw the attention of the enemy to allow James an opportunity to pick off the remaining Spetsnaz soldier.

He ducked for cover a shred of a second before the Russian opened fire. The Cuban heard bullets hammer his rocky shelter. Encizo sucked in a tense breath as Calvin James settled his M-16 on the Soviet trooper. He triggered three more rounds and hit the enemy gunman in the throat and upper chest, kicking him off his feet. The Spetsnaz tumbled over rocks and slithered into a shallow dip that was half-filled with water. By the time the Phoenix warriors reached the spot, the Russian was lying facedown in the water, his blood tingeing it a dirty pink.

"That was a reckless move, Rafael," Katz said a little sternly.

"Got the job done," Encizo replied.

"I agree," James said. "But it wasn't the kind of thing I expected to see coming from you."

Encizo shrugged, glancing over James's shoulder at McCarter.

"Must be something to do with the company I keep," he said.

McCarter barely managed to hold back a hoot of laughter. He shook his head as he turned away and continued on along the canyon. "Come on, you guys," he said. "If the sound of those shots reached the guerrilla base, we may already have lost our surprise element."

"He's right," Katz said. "Let's speed things up."

21

Out on the heaving swell of the Pacific, events were already moving at a faster pace.

Within minutes of launching the CH-53 helicopter on its planned retrieval flight, the USS *Anaconda*'s captain received information that the carrier's radar had picked up the presence of a large vessel on a confrontation course.

Captain Garner spoke to his officer over the bridge phone. "What do you think it is, Jerry?"

"By her size and estimated speed, Captain, I'd say our Russian counterpart. Most likely the carrier *Chekov* our friend Roskov took off from."

"Any sign of her putting any aircraft up?"

"Nothing yet, sir."

"Keep her on-screen, Jerry. I want to know every move that ship makes. If her captain goes to the can I want to know."

"Will do, Captain."

"DO YOU THINK the American carrier will have picked us up by now?" Tchenko asked.

The *Chekov*'s captain nodded. "There is no doubt," he said.

Tchenko looked pleased and smoothed his hands down his clothes as though to keep from rubbing them together. "Good. Then they will have realized that we are not playing games."

"I doubt they ever saw this matter as a game," the captain said. He was becoming increasingly troubled about Tchenko's attitude. The KGB man seemed to be willing something to happen. "The Americans do not take this sort of thing lightly."

"Of course not," Tchenko replied. "Neither do I. This is serious. The Americans have interfered with what is an internal Soviet matter. We are perfectly justified in taking whatever action we feel necessary to put it right."

"To what extremes?" asked the captain.

"That will depend on how far the Americans are prepared to go."

"If they feel they have been pushed too far, they might commit themselves to direct action. Have you thought about that?"

"Certainly," Tchenko answered. "We have the ability to face fire with fire. Do we not, Captain?"

"If I choose to use it," the captain said.

"The choice may not be yours to make," Tchenko corrected. "Please remember who has the final word over this. This is still a KGB operation."

The captain was wishing he could forget the KGB. He just wanted Tchenko to go away. He also knew that was not going to happen.

"Isn't it time we thought about launching our helicopter?" the KGB man asked. "The sooner we get it airborne, the better our chances of picking up the

Barracuda before those damn Americans try the same thing."

"I will see what the flight controller feels about the weather conditions."

Left alone for a while, Tchenko stared out of the bridge windows. Rain sheeted across the heavy Pacific swell. The wind whipped the waves to white froth. The vast bulk of the carrier was hardly affected by the turmoil. It plowed on through the mountainous sea, keeping its course toward the Guatemalan coast, and more importantly, the American carrier already in the area.

Tchenko knew he had to gain the upper hand. He could not allow the Americans to snatch the Barracuda from under his very nose. If that did happen, his career would come to an abrupt end. Tchenko was a loyal KGB man. But being something of an insider meant that he understood the way the KGB worked, and especially how failure was rewarded. He had no intention of letting that happen. No matter what it cost.

22

Another half mile lay ahead of Phoenix Force before they reached the point in the canyon where the floor rose in a long slope to peter out on a rock-strewn, broken ridge.

The Force moved cautiously to the ridge, flattening out on their stomachs to peer over the summit.

They saw that they had reached their goal.

The guerrilla base was situated in a wide natural basin, with a high rock escarpment forming an impenetrable barrier on the perimeter beyond.

Spread out across the far side of the floor of the basin was a haphazard collection of wood and adobe huts of varying sizes. Untidy stacks of packing cases and other odds and ends were scattered about the area.

In front of the largest hut was a sandbagged gun emplacement with a Russian 7.62 mm PKM machine gun being manhandled into place.

Men were to be seen moving around the compound fronting the huts. The distinctive spotted camou fatigues of the Soviet soldiers stood out among the FAR guerrillas' less formal wear. Both Russians and Guatemalans were alike in one instance—to a man, they were all armed.

Encizo touched Katz on the shoulder. "There," he said, pointing something out to the Israeli. "Radio shack. See the antenna?"

Katz nodded. "We could do to have control of that," he acknowledged. "Rafael, you and David make that one of your priorities."

"How do we handle this?" James asked.

"No time for niceties," the Phoenix commander said, watching the movement of the base's occupants. "The way they're chasing around down there suggests that company is expected."

"Let's not disappoint them," McCarter said.

"All I want to see is Gary—alive and well," James declared.

"Don't we all," McCarter added. "Funny, isn't it," the brash Cockney added, "but I miss his ugly mug."

"Cal, drop a couple of rounds down there," Katz suggested. "When they detonate, we go in."

"You got it," James answered.

He pulled a pair of M-406 High Explosive 40 mm rounds from his webbing and loaded one into the M-203 grenade launcher mounted under his M-16's barrel. The black warrior selected his area and eased back the M-203's trigger. While the first grenade was still in the air, James loaded and fired the second canister. The HE rounds rose and fell, dropping rapidly toward the distant compound.

In the seconds before the grenades exploded, Phoenix Force prepared to move down off the ridge. They saw the grenades detonate within moments of each other. The dull thud of the HE rounds, followed by twin geysers of muddy earth and dirty smoke, caused some confusion among the base defenders, and two men were laid low by flying fragments.

The time was right to meet the enemy head-on.

"GO!" KATZ SAID. The Israeli followed Calvin James over the ridge, finding that the soft, rain-soaked earth restricted movement. The mud clung to his boots, slowing him. Ahead of him James found the same problem. The only consolation lay in the fact that the base defenders would also encounter the same hardship.

Neither of the Phoenix warriors allowed the conditions to defeat him. They plunged down the slope toward the compound, guns set and ready. James had managed to load a third HE round in the final moment before moving out.

The first sighting of the Phoenix warriors was by one of the Spetsnaz troops. The Russian, in a forward position, had been well clear of the exploding HE rounds. He had stopped in his tracks at the time of the explosions, glancing back over his shoulder in time to see the bursts. Aware of the implication of the detonations, the Soviet specialist scanned the approach to the basin, deciding that if an attack was imminent it would be from that direction.

His intuition proved correct. He spotted four armed, camou-clad figures moving down toward the compound. The group had split into pairs. The closest to his position was a black man, closely followed by a shorter, older man.

The Russian raised his Kalashnikov, tracking the muzzle around to pick up the older man, who appeared to be moving at a slower pace than the younger black man.

A crackle of gunfire disturbed the Russian's concentration. In the same moment, he experienced a tearing sensation in his chest. The sudden pain was followed by a terrific impact that knocked the Russian flat on his back in the mud. His finger jerked back against the trigger of his AK-47, sending a burst of 7.62 mm slugs into the rain-streaked sky.

The shots from James's M-16 acted as a signal. The compound erupted with gunfire. A number of the Guatemalan guerrillas were firing blind, still panicked by the grenade explosions. They opened up out of sheer tension, not even taking aim.

Katz, scanning the area, picked up on a guerrilla taking aim at him. Without breaking his stride, the Israeli swung the barrel of his Uzi and triggered a burst that stitched across the rebel's right arm and shoulder and into his chest. Still on the move, Katz turned his SMG at a guerrilla charging across the compound. The Guatemalan, heavily built and broad across the shoulders, carried an AK-47 fitted with a folding metal butt. He opened fire as he closed in on the Israeli, spraying the air with 7.62 mm slugs. He began to yell incoherently, as if he expected the noise to improve his aim. Keeping his head, Katz dropped the Uzi's muzzle a fraction and touched the trigger, sending 9 mm slugs into the rebel's body. The guerrilla grunted with shock as he fell to his knees, then pitched facedown in the mud.

Even as Katz was taking out his targets, Calvin James found himself confronted by a threesome of Russian Spetsnaz. The Soviet specialists came at

James from the drifting smoke left by the exploding grenades. One had a bloody tear in the sleeve of his camou jacket, evidence of his close escape from serious injury. As the Soviets emerged from the smoke, their gaze settled on the American commando. They brought up their weapons, needing only a split second to zero in on their target. But they didn't get a chance. Calvin James, already way ahead of them mentally, had pulled back the M-16's trigger, sending 3-round bursts into them. The Spetsnaz were stopped in their tracks by the hot projectiles, their bodies jerking in an ungainly dance, arms flailing wildly. James emptied his magazine into the trio, making sure they were going to stay down. The moment he fired the last shot, he slipped his finger into the triggerguard of the grenade launcher, triggering the load in the direction of a bunch of Guatemalan Communist guerrillas he'd spotted emerging from behind one of the huts. The four rebels were blown out of the fight in a hellish moment of heat and light as the HE grenade tore at their flesh, leaving them numbed and bleeding in the mud.

Both Katz and James found they had broken through the line of defense at this point. They reached one of the outlying huts and sought cover against the front wall. James had slotted in a fresh magazine during the run for the hut. Now he cocked the M-16 and sent 3-round bursts in the direction of guerrillas and Spetsnaz alike, scattering the surprised force.

THE PRESENCE of McCarter and Encizo added to the confusion. They, like Katz and James, had come down off the ridge in the moments after the two grenades had exploded, bursting in among the base defenders like hot knives slicing through butter.

McCarter needed no second bidding. The Briton, as always, charged in without a moment's hesitation. He was up and over the ridge before Encizo, but the fiery Cuban followed within seconds.

They cut across the open compound, splashing through puddles of rainwater, the ground beneath their feet soft mud.

Figures broke from cover ahead of them, their weapons swinging up to cover the Phoenix pair. The rattle of autofire erupted into the steadily monotonous pattering of the downpour. Bullets scythed the air around McCarter and Encizo.

McCarter returned fire, his KG-99 spitting a stream of 9 mm slugs that slapped one Guatemalan off his feet and dumped him facedown in the mud. The instant he had fired the Briton turned and triggered a second burst at another advancing figure. His spray of bullets struck a second before Encizo's. The unlucky guerrilla caught slugs in the chest and the stomach that ripped the life from him. He crashed to the ground in a tangle of loose limbs.

Side by side, the Phoenix warriors raced on, still firing. They took out the last rebel a few yards from the hut. The Guatemalan fell to the ground, yelling loudly as he clutched both hands to the bloody hole in his chest.

Encizo flattened himself against the wall, sleeving rainwater from his face, his eyes searching the way ahead.

"Nothing like a good run in the fresh air to keep you healthy," McCarter observed as he joined Encizo.

The Cuban pointed at the semicircle of sandbags, behind which squatted three Guatemalans and their 7.62 mm PKM machine gun. They were busily feeding an ammunition belt into the weapon. From their position the rebels would be able to cover the entire front area of the base, including the trail that ended at the compound. "That won't do much for your health," he said.

McCarter glanced in the direction of the machine gun. "Got it in one, mate," he agreed.

In the distance autofire crackled briefly, fell silent, then sounded again.

"Katz and Cal?" McCarter wondered.

"We'd better keep our end up," Encizo said.

He turned swiftly, his MP-5 erupting with sound, and some distance away a guerrilla figure kicked over onto his back as Encizo's 9 mm shredders crashed into his chest. McCarter swung his KG-99 toward the fallen figure, but held his fire when it was obvious the man was already dead.

"Sneaky buggers, aren't they?" McCarter remarked.

"Can't trust them," the Cuban agreed as he swapped magazines in the MP-5. "How do you want to handle the machine gun nest?"

"I'd like them to surrender," McCarter replied as he took a fragmentation grenade from his belt, "but I don't reckon they'll oblige."

"Too far away to throw that grenade," Encizo stated.

"Not if I get closer," the Briton declared. "Cover me."

Encizo was about to protest but realized it was a waste of time. He fired at the machine gun nest, deliberately aiming high to allow McCarter to break cover and rush toward the sandbags in a low crouch. The Cuban saw the enemy duck beneath their shelter as he triggered the H&K volley. He hoped they would be distracted well enough not to notice McCarter.

The Briton ran forward and yanked the pin from his M-26 fragger. He clutched the grenade in his fist to hold the spoon down and dove for a tree trunk about twenty yards from the PKM stronghold. McCarter rolled to cover and popped the lever to arm the grenade. He held it for a two-count and prepared to throw the explosive egg.

Machine gun fire ripped into the tree and chewed bark from McCarter's shelter. He yanked back his arm in time to avoid getting it torn off by the high-velocity bullets. The Briton's gut twisted, aware he had a live grenade in his fist that was about to explode in one second.

Encizo fired, spraying the front sandbags with parabellum slugs. The enemy swung their PKM death machine at the Cuban's position and blasted a short burst. The Cuban ducked behind cover as bullets raked the adobe wall. The men behind the sandbags shifted the aim of the machine gun back to its original position, dragging the ammunition belt with it.

But by then Encizo had ranged in. He touched off another burst from the MP-5, a number of his 9 mm slugs catching the belt feeder in the side of the head. The stricken guerrilla tumbled out of sight, still clutching the belt and making the weapon jerk off target.

Taking advantage of the confusion, McCarter delivered his grenade. It arced through the air and dropped behind the sandbags, unnoticed by the remaining members of the machine gun crew. They remained in ignorance until the grenade exploded and ripped the life from their shredded bodies.

Encizo crouched with McCarter beside the tumbled sandbags as they surveyed the area.

"That's it," McCarter said, indicating the hut and the tall antenna that had been erected beside it. Before they moved off, the Briton fed a fresh magazine into his KG-99. "Let's go," he urged.

Encizo provided cover as McCarter headed for the radio shack. Reaching the shelter of the front wall, McCarter waved Encizo forward, then took his turn to shield his partner's dash.

When the Cuban reached his objective, he pressed his ear to the door. He heard voices inside the shack, and it sounded as though they were Russian.

The Cuban tapped McCarter's shoulder to attract his attention. "At least two," he said.

McCarter nodded. Encizo turned to the door, raised his right foot and kicked the door open. As it sprang back against the inside wall, McCarter went in, thrusting the KG-99 before him.

There was one Spetsnaz seated at the wooden table on which rested a radio set. A second Soviet stood beside the table, his AK-47 held at the ready. He turned to face the door as it crashed open, seeking a target with his Kalashnikov.

The KG-99 in McCarter's hands stuttered sharply, hurling 9 mm death at the Spetsnaz. The Russian stumbled back against the wall, and a stunned expression showed in his eyes as the slugs burned deep into his chest. He coughed harshly, spitting frothy blood as he slithered loosely down the wall.

Encizo, who had stepped into the hut behind McCarter, found his attention drawn to the radio operator.

As McCarter had burst into the hut, the operator had tossed aside his microphone, making a grab for the 9 mm Makarov pistol lying on the table. He barely had time to touch the butt before a short burst from Encizo's MP-5 knocked him of his seat. The radioman crashed to the floor, his limbs jerking in uncontrolled spasms.

"Shut that ruddy door," McCarter growled as he picked up the microphone.

Encizo closed the door and stayed beside it so he could keep an eye on what was going on outside while McCarter began to check through all the radio frequencies. "What are you doing?" Encizo asked.

"Just playing the field," McCarter answered. "You never know what we might pick up."

All he appeared to be picking up was a lot of static. Once he tuned in to a conversation in Russian, glancing at Encizo as the words came through the loudspeaker.

The Cuban shrugged. "Don't ask me. I'm still having trouble understanding you."

"Ha-bloody-ha," McCarter said, adjusting the frequency settings again. This time he picked up an American voice.

"It's Jack Grimaldi," Encizo said.

"What?" McCarter asked.

"Listen," Encizo said. "It *is* Jack."

McCarter snatched up the microphone. He depressed the button. "Phoenix to Dragon Slayer. Phoenix to Dragon Slayer. Come in, Dragon Slayer. Do you read me? Over."

Grimaldi's voice, tinged with obvious relief, came over the radio. "Where the hell are you guys?"

"Right in the middle of the enemy camp," McCarter explained. "We could do with some extra firepower down here, Jack. How about it?"

"I'm on my way," Grimaldi replied. "Trouble is, this storm is making it hard for me to pinpoint the rebel base."

"Can we do anything?"

"Leave the radio on transmit. I'll home in on the signal."

"How long?" McCarter wanted to know.

"Give me a minute to punch in to the computer," the Stony Man pilot explained.

"Hey, we got company on the way," Encizo warned. "Couple of our Russian buddies."

McCarter nodded. "Hey, Jack, got to go. We're going to get visitors, and they won't be from the Fuller Brush Company."

"Okay, Phoenix," Grimaldi said. "Be dropping in soon as I can. Over and out."

McCarter placed the microphone on the table, wedging the microphone against the radio set so the transmit button would remain depressed. He picked up his KG-99.

"Here we go again," he grumbled. "Busy, busy."

23

A niggling thought kept vying for Kirov's attention. He tried ignoring it, but it persisted, and finally the Spetsnaz commander turned toward the hut where the American specialist was being held.

As his hand touched the door catch, Kirov knew what he would find. His suspicions were confirmed as the door swung open.

The prisoner was gone.

Karamatsov lay on the floor, a pool of dark blood congealing around his head. Nearby, the Spetsnaz who had been guarding the American lay trussed up.

Kirov immediately turned away, keeping close to the front of the hut, running in the direction of the hut where Roskov was detained. Even as he approached, he saw that the guard wasn't on duty outside the hut.

The Soviet's control evaporated into wild, unreasoning fury as he realized the implications of allowing his prisoners to escape. He inwardly raged at the circumstances that had forced him into his present position, circumstances beyond his control and certainly beyond the sphere of his influence.

His bitterness was directed at the KGB. The damn KGB and their twisted schemes. The spy masters back in Moscow, safe and protected behind their multilevel organization, issued directives that decided the fate of individuals thousands of miles distant. If a plan worked, the spy masters took the credit. If it failed, they laid the blame on some luckless person who didn't even have the right to challenge his accusers.

Kirov pictured that to be his own fate. The failure of the operation would need an accounting, and as unit commander, he would be responsible.

The injustice of the situation only served to fuel Kirov's rage. He raced toward Roskov's hut, oblivious to the firefight going on around him. He smashed the door open with his shoulder, charging into the hut, finding it deserted except for the bound and gagged guard. A probing glance revealed to him the gaping hole in the hut's rear wall.

Kirov sprang to the opening, then pushed his way through the gap. He scanned the area outside, noticed the the double set of footprints in the soft earth and began to follow them.

Ejecting the partly used magazine from his AK-47, Kirov fed a fresh one into the weapon. He needed to find the escapees, as much for his own satisfaction as to meet the real need to rescue the operation from utter failure.

The boot prints were still well formed, not yet having had time to fill with rainwater or crumble around the edges. That indicated they had been made very recently.

There was movement at the edge of a hut. Kirov glanced up and saw Lieutenant Roskov's face as the Russian pilot tried to duck behind the shelter. The Spetsnaz commander fired his Kalashnikov from the hip. Bullets punched into adobe, and dust spit from the wall as Roskov cried out. Kirov held his AK-47 ready and jogged to the edge of the hut. He found Roskov sprawled on the ground, a hand clutched to his bloodied, bullet-torn right arm. The Russian pilot looked up at Kirov, his eyes filled with pain and fear, yet a glimmer of defiance remained.

"Where is the American?" Kirov demanded in Russian. "Answer me, you traitor, or I'll shoot you through both legs and your testicles and leave you to die slowly and in terrible agony. You won't even die as a man...."

"Drop it, Kirov!" a voice shouted in English. "The game's over and you lose!"

The captain raised his head and saw Manning emerge from behind a stack of packing crates, the AK-47 in his fists pointed at Kirov. The Spetsnaz officer realized he couldn't swing his own rifle at the Canadian and open fire before Manning took him out. Kirov released the pistol grip of his Kalashnikov and held the rifle by the barrel in one fist as he extended his arm to the side.

"The game is over," Kirov stated with a nod, and dropped the AK.

His other hand clawed at his Makarov pistol and yanked it from leather as he dropped to one knee. Kirov started to point the pistol when Manning triggered his Kalashnikov. Three 7.62 mm slugs chopped through Kirov's torso. The impact spun him around to receive another trio of full-auto rounds between the shoulder blades. The Soviet commando boss fell against the adobe wall. He still held the Makarov in his fist, but could not find the strength to raise it as he stared at Gary Manning. Kirov let the pistol fall and uttered something that resembled a laugh. Blood gurgled from his lips, and he slumped lifeless and lay still in the filthy mud of a Guatemalan rebel base.

Manning turned back to Roskov. He shoved back the Russian's sleeve and inspected his arm. A couple of bullets had torn deep grooves in the flesh, and they were bleeding badly.

The Canadian opened his camou jacket and slipped it off. He removed his T-shirt, then replaced his jacket. After he tore the T-shirt apart, he made a pad to cover the wounds, then used the remaining strips of the shirt to bind the pad tightly in place.

"Can't do any more at the moment," he said. "I need to make contact with my teammates. One of them is a medic."

Manning picked up the AK-47 Roskov had dropped and thrust it into the Russian's hand. "Hang on to this. If you see trouble coming, use it. I'll be back quick as I can."

Roskov sat with his back to the wall of the hut. "I will be all right," he said.

Manning nodded. He slipped away from the rear of the hut, making his way in the direction of the compound, where the firefight was still going on. He knew now that his Phoenix partners were out there and he needed to join them. It had been a great moment, looking out through the crack in the door of the hut and recognizing the members of the Stony Man team. He had also seen Kirov storming out of the first hut and making his way toward Manning and Roskov's temporary refuge. The Canadian hadn't wanted to find himself trapped in the confines of a small hut, so he and Roskov had kicked out a couple of the back-wall timbers and had made a quick exit.

Now it was time to rejoin Phoenix Force.

24

The battle was far from over.

The combined Spetsnaz-guerrilla unit had scattered in order to regroup. Phoenix Force's all-out attack had cut through the base defenders with devastating effect. The Stony Man warriors' relentless combat thrust swept aside everything in its path. Even the battle-hardened Soviet troops wilted before the fury of the Phoenix commandos.

With the first line of base defenders all but taken out, the Phoenix team had a brief respite as the Russians and their Guatemalan partners drew back. Others, who had been posted to the farthest perimeter of the base, came hurrying back in the direction of the huts.

Katz and James, their backs to the wall of a hut, reloaded and prepared to face the next attack.

It was the Phoenix commander who caught a glimpse of two Guatemalan rebels sneaking along the back of a line of empty weapons cases. The end of the line of cases lay only ten feet from the hut where Katz and James had paused. The Israeli saw the rebels' strategy. They would stay under cover until they reached the end of the line of cases, then launch their attack.

"Cal, watch my back," the Israeli said, easing away from the wall of the hut and moving across open ground.

Katz came into line with the row of cases, and from there he also saw the two Guatemalan Communists.

One of them raised his head, which he had been keeping low so as not to be spotted above the wooden cases. He came face-to-face with Katz. The guerrilla yelled a startled warning to his companion. Both rebels began to raise their AK-47's.

The 9 mm Uzi in Katz's hand, braced across his prosthesis, opened up with a deadly chatter, spewing hot slugs into the rebels. They were caught in the stream of autofire and tossed across the muddy compound in a brief dance of death. One triggered his AK-47, finger stiffening on the trigger. The barrel of the Soviet assault rifle hosed the area with uncontrolled fire.

As the Guatemalans tumbled to the muddy earth, Katz ran into the cover of the line of crates himself, using them to extend his killing ground. He moved quickly along the line, eyes and ears tuned for any sound above the pouring rain.

When he reached the far end of the line, Katz was in time to see a bunch of rebels climbing up from a depression in the ground. One issued orders to the others, and they began to spread out as they moved forward.

The Israeli did not hesitate. He leaned out from his flimsy cover, triggering the Uzi in the direction of the group. His first blast of 9 mm slugs crashed into the chest of the two guerrillas in the lead, sending them tumbling back against their comrades and scattering the group.

One of the rebels, quicker to recover than his comrades, turned an AK-47 in Katz's direction and opened up with full-auto fire.

The Israeli ducked back behind the cases, hearing the 7.62 mm slugs chewing the wood to shreds amid a shower of splinters.

Instead of retreating, Katz did the opposite, stepping away from the cases to face the group, who were reorganizing themselves. He triggered the Uzi again, this time arcing the SMG back and forth. Burning slugs hammered at the rebels, tearing through flesh and splintering bones. The Guatemalans' dreams of Marxist supremacy dissolved in mists of blood as they were terminated with brutal finality.

Katz heard the sound of James's grenade launcher. Seconds later one of the huts exploded in a mushroom of shattered timber and crumbling adobe. Out of the debris tumbled the bodies of two Spetsnaz, one still clutching the RPG-7 rocket launcher he had been about to use. James followed his grenade launch with a burst of M-16 fire that ensured the Soviets stayed down.

The Israeli fed a fresh magazine into his Uzi, racking back the bolt to cock the weapon, then turned and made his way back along the line of packing cases. The sound of autofire from the other side of the compound indicated that there was still business taking place in that area, as well.

GARY MANNING ROUNDED the corner of the hut, eyes scanning the compound for signs of his Phoenix partners.

His gaze was drawn to a pair of Spetsnaz troopers closing in on the base's radio shack.

As the Canadian watched, he saw the door to the radio shack ease partway open. A tall figure in camou fatigues peered out, spotted the approaching Russians, and jerked back inside. The door closed.

The image had been brief, but there had been enough time for Manning to recognize the unmistakable features of David McCarter.

The Spetsnaz separated, weapons up as they closed the distance to the hut. One Soviet snatched a grenade from his webbing, pulling the pin.

Manning triggered his AK-47, putting a short burst into the Russian. The Spetsnaz was driven to his knees as the 7.62 mm slugs chewed into his body. He lost his grip on the grenade, and it dropped into the mud a short distance away from the wounded man.

The Russian's partner turned on his heel, his Kalashnikov seeking a target.

Manning took him out with a second blast, stitching the Soviet from stomach to throat. The Spetsnaz twisted in agony, arching over onto his back, his legs thrashing as he hit the ground. The blood bubbling from his lacerated chest turned to pink froth as the rain pounded against him.

The grenade detonated with a roar, the blast shredding the wounded Russian's body in an instant.

Manning ran across to the radio shack. He pounded on the door with the butt of his Kalashnikov.

"Open up, you crazy Cockney," he declared. "It's your long-lost brother."

"Bite your tongue." The reply came from the edge of the building.

Manning turned to stare into the grinning, foxlike face of David McCarter. The Canadian had to resist an urge to embrace his fellow Phoenix pro, but he would have been embarrassed. McCarter would never let him live it down. Manning didn't realize that the British ace's thoughts and feelings were identical to his own.

"You look bloody awful," McCarter commented when he got a good look at Manning's battered face.

"Yeah," Manning said with a weak grin. "You should see the other guy. He's dead."

ENCIZO AND MCCARTER had left the radio shack via the rear door. They had noticed Manning headed for the hut. The Cuban had gestured for McCarter to go get their Canadian partner while he stayed at the rear of the shack to cover them.

Suddenly two men appeared from another hut, both clad in the ragtag manner of the FAR terrorists. In fact one was Salazar, the terrorist cell leader. They spotted Encizo at the same moment the Cuban swung his MP-5 at the pair and opened fire.

Hot lead tore into Salazar's companion and ripped open his ribcage to expose a mess of splintered bone. Keen shards found their way into his heart and lungs. He collapsed in a slithering heap as Salazar raised his PPS submachine gun to return fire.

Encizo shifted the aim of his H&K chopper and triggered the last two rounds from the subgun's magazine. Salazar cried out and started to spin about from the force of the high-velocity projectiles that plowed into his right shoulder and biceps. The Soviet-made PPS flew from the terrorist leader's grasp. Encizo held the MP-5 by the frame with one hand and reached for his pistol in shoulder leather with the other.

Salazar suddenly bellowed like a furious beast and charged at Encizo. His right arm dangled uselessly by his side, but he pulled a machete from a belt sheath with his left hand as he closed in. The long jungle knife slashed at Encizo and forced him to jump back to avoid the heavy blade.

The Cuban slammed the frame of his MP-5 into the machete to parry the big knife as he drew the P-9S autoloader from the shoulder rig. Salazar hooked a front elbow-smash to Encizo's forearm and struck the pistol from numb fingers. The FAR *jefe* slashed his machete in a cross-body stroke, determined to chop Encizo's head off.

The Phoenix warrior blocked the heavy blade once more with the H&K in his left fist and quickly snatched his Cold Steel Tanto from its belt sheath. He drove the tip of the knife blade under Salazar's ribs and cut upward in a curved motion that outlined the form of his ribcage, carving a vicious gash to the base of Salazar's sternum. The terrorist screamed as Encizo shoved him backward before he could swing his machete at close quarters.

Blood gushed from Salazar's torso as he dropped his machete to clasp his hand to the wound to stem the flow. He stared at Encizo as his knees buckled and he dropped to the ground. Salazar tried to speak, but blood filled his throat. Crimson drool spilled from the FAR goon's mouth, and he fell facefirst in the mud.

"Jesus," Manning remarked as he and McCarter jogged from the front of the shack to join Encizo. "You okay, Rafael?"

"I'm doing a lot better than he is," Encizo answered, and pointed at Salazar's corpse with the blood-stained blade of his Tanto. "If you two have finished the reunion rituals, we still have a little war here."

"Right," McCarter said cheerfully. "Let's do it."

25

Jack Grimaldi had no trouble locating the enemy base. The tracking equipment on Dragon Slayer guided him to the area, and the glare of automatic weapons and exploding grenades below left no doubt he had found the proper site. The storm had subsided, and Grimaldi flew over the clearing with ease. The infrared searchlight allowed him to handle the chopper in the darkness while watching the night screen. Dragon Slayer hovered above the battlefield like a great dark bat.

He applied slow, gradual pressure on the collective controls, and the helicopter began to descend. Weapons opened fire at the mighty aircraft. Grimaldi had no doubt the gunfire had to be from the enemy side. Phoenix Force would not mistake Dragon Slayer for a Soviet copter. The Stony Man pilot aimed the rotary cannon at the shadowy attackers and opened fire. Dragon Slayer bellowed with fearsome firepower. The infrared screen revealed several opponents toppling like tenpins from the fury of the gunship's hardware.

Grimaldi saw two figures head for Dragon Slayer. They carried weapons, but fired at shapes within the compound and did not direct their gun barrels at Grimaldi's airship. The pilot recognized the tall black man and the one-armed Israeli as they hurried to the chopper. Grimaldi put the controls in full-down position to land the copter.

"Hurry up!" the pilot shouted as he opened a sliding door. "One grenade launcher can put me out of business forever!"

Calvin James and Yakov Katzenelenbogen rushed to the side of the chopper, but didn't climb aboard until they saw Gary Manning and David McCarter jog for the Dragon Slayer with Lieutenant Roskov between them. They half carried, half dragged the wounded Russian pilot. Rafael Encizo brought up the rear and covered them. The Cuban fired at the surrounding enemies to keep them at bay until Manning and McCarter could haul Roskov to the door of Grimaldi's gunship.

"Welcome aboard," Grimaldi greeted. He was relieved to see that Manning and Roskov were still alive.

"Jack!" Manning exclaimed. "I was afraid you bought the farm when you went off that ridge with that FAR half-wit."

"I came close enough to consider retirement," Grimaldi replied, although he knew nobody would believe him. Least of all himself. "Close that door. We're going up!"

Encizo jumped aboard last and slammed the door shut as Grimaldi raised the collective controls and opened the throttle to full power. Dragon Slayer rose swiftly into the air. The super pilot checked his night screen and shifted the aim of the rotary cannon to rake another salvo of blazing destruction on the enemy below. The hazing fire was simply to convince the remaining Spetsnaz and FAR terrorists to stay back as the helicopter climbed higher and finally swung above the treetops.

"Figure they've had enough?" Grimaldi inquired as he worked the rudders and cyclic controls to steer the chopper to the right.

"They don't have any aircraft down there or any antiaircraft firepower that we noticed," Katz answered. "There's no need to hit them again. The Spetsnaz are, after all, following orders. They're soldiers and don't deserve to be slaughtered simply because they were given immoral commands by whoever ordered this operation."

"A couple of those Russian soldiers were a little too enthusiastic to deserve any sympathy," Manning commented dryly. "But I already settled the score with them. For what it's worth, Rafael took out the leader of the FAR terrorists, as well."

"Let's be careful about using names too freely," Encizo suggested as he tilted his head toward Roskov. "Don't forget about security."

"Don't worry," Calvin James assured him. The Phoenix medic knelt beside Roskov and cut open the pilot's sleeve to examine his wounds. "This dude is out cold. He sure ain't gonna be pitching for the major leagues with this arm, but he's not gonna lose it."

"Is there internal bleeding?" Manning inquired.

"Doesn't seem to be," James answered. "Roskov's wing will be in a sling for a while, but he ought to be okay. Really should get him to a hospital as soon as possible just in case my snap diagnosis is off base."

"Well, I need to know where we're headed here," Grimaldi announced. "We go back to the *Anaconda*, or do you want to try to get Barracuda out of the jungle and in the air? I'll tell ya, that didn't look all that likely when I last saw the MiG."

"Is it damaged?" McCarter inquired.

"Barracuda seemed to be in perfect working order," Grimaldi answered, "but I don't know how the hell you're gonna taxi it through the rain forest. The Spetsnaz and Guatemalan goons had tried to cut a path through the jungle, but that would take days to make enough space to use for an improvised runway."

"That depends what method you use to cut a path," Manning commented. He looked at Katz and Encizo. "Do you guys have any plastic explosives? Primacord and detonators?"

"We packed extra just for you," Encizo assured him. "A *bandito* bastard named Jorge kindly allowed us to take as much as we wanted from a supply he had at his camp."

"Let me see what we've got," Manning urged. "Maybe we can get Barracuda out of the jungle, after all."

"You figure out a way for me to get her rolling forward a hundred yards or so," McCarter declared, "and I'll get her in the air."

"This is a new aircraft, David," Encizo said, and shook his head. "We might be better off destroying it rather than risk flying a MiG you've never handled before."

"I've logged close to three hundred hours in a confiscated MiG-25 when I was with the SAS," McCarter announced. "I've also used a simulator of the M-27 and I'm familiar with the controls. Barracuda's basically a glorified MiG-27. Right?"

"As near as I could tell," Grimaldi confirmed. "Barracuda is about fifty-three feet long with a wing-span around forty-six feet. Same general dimensions as the MiG-27. It probably weighs about forty thousand pounds. If the ground is muddied badly enough from the storm, you'll never get a plane that heavy out of there by flying her."

"We'll just have to see what we can do," Katz stated. "Jack, fly to Barracuda. We'll see if we can get to the plane, and if so, you can drop off David, Gary, Rafael and me. Cal should stay with Roskov until you get him to the *Anaconda*. They certainly have a dispensary there."

"On an aircraft carrier?" James said with a chuckle. "Hell, they've got a major hospital with a full staff. Aircraft carriers are like floating cities, man. They got everything except a brothel on one of those monster rigs."

"Excuse me," Katz said with a shrug. "I was never in the navy."

"Okay," Grimaldi began, as he reached for the handset to his radio. "I'd better contact *Anaconda* and tell them enough details so they don't send out choppers with crane lifts to try pull out Barracuda unless you guys can't manage this little miracle. The airlift would be a great idea if it wasn't for the fact the Guatemalan authorities are probably already looking into what's been going on off their coast. If they see a parade of choppers head inland, they might figure the U.S. has launched an invasion."

"What about the Russians?" James inquired. "You figure they'll just sit out on their aircraft carrier and calmly watch us take off with Barracuda?"

"More or less," Katz replied. "The Spetsnaz troops were already here working with the Guatemalan fanatics with some sort of covert KGB scheme that nobody in Moscow will ever admit to being part of. The Soviets have lost Barracuda and Roskov. That sort of thing happens all the time in the Cold War. Trying to reclaim the MiG or get Roskov back would simply present too many high risks with too much to lose to make it worth the potential gain of succeeding. The Soviets won't take this any further unless they've got a lunatic in charge."

MAJOR TCHENKO STOOD at portside of the *Chekov*. He stared at the dawn sky. Daybreak came abruptly. He squinted his small eyes, since the sudden brightness came as a start. Tchenko did not like the bright sun and tropical climate. He favored the cold weather of Mother Russia in the dead of winter. Tchenko believed jungle climates produced jungle mentalities. Such weather was suited for savages, not for civilized and intelligent men such as himself.

He wore a flight suit, complete with parachute and underarm life preserver on his right side. The rip cord to the chute was under the left arm. Tchenko's helmet was fitted over a skull cap with an oxygen mask, complete with built-in microphone, clipped to one side of the headgear. A combination oxygen hose and mike lead hung across the left side of his chest like a rubber snake.

Tchenko's thoughts were grim and brooding as he considered the radio message from Lieutenant Litinov. They had received the junior officer's report less than an hour earlier. He had announced that Captain

Kirov and most of the Spetsnaz troops had been killed in a fierce gunbattle with a commando strike force that successfully rescued the remaining American spy and that damn traitor Roskov. Salazar and nearly all the FAR guerrilla followers were also dead. Litinov requested permission to gather the surviving members of his unit and return to the *Pushkin* so they could rendezvous with the Soviet carrier. Since the Spetsnaz operation was obviously ruined, Tchenko agreed to the suggestion.

However, Litinov's statement that he had ordered the men guarding the Barracuda to leave their post and return to base to join the other troops infuriated Tchenko. The lieutenant had not had the good sense to order them to blow up the MiG before they abandoned the site. Now the Americans would be able to claim the fighter jet, as well as the pilot. Tchenko would have to decide whether or not to have Litinov shot for this blunder.

Now there was only one option left, in the KGB officer's opinion. He could not return to Moscow and report this failure. Not after he ordered the Spetsnaz troops into action and got most of them killed trying to keep Barracuda and Roskov from falling into the hands of the Americans. At the very least Tchenko had to stop them from claiming Barracuda.

This time he would supervise the task himself. Tchenko had ordered a squad of MiG-27 fighters to be prepared—with the best pilots aboard the *Chekov*—to take off as soon as possible. Major Tchenko would personally lead the squadron. He was a qualified fighter pilot himself, although he had not flown a mission since 1981 in Afghanistan. Tchenko was more than willing to get into the cockpit of a MiG once more and blow Barracuda to hell. If any Americans or U.S. aircraft happened to be in the way, he had no objections to destroying them also.

Captain Zimin approached the KGB major, accompanied by three of his officers. Tchenko grunted with annoyance, aware the captain would object to his issuing commands without any consultation.

Zimin stood before Tchenko and put his hands on his hips as he fixed the KGB man with a hard stare. "I have revoked your orders, Major," he announced. "This whole affair has gone far enough. You have cost the lives of enough Soviet soldiers. My crew are not going to contribute to the body count."

"When we return to the Soviet Union, I will have you brought up on charges," Tchenko told him. "This is treason and a conspiracy against the state. You'll spend the rest of your life in a Siberian labor camp if you continue to interfere with my mission. Is that clear, Captain?"

"Threatening me under these circumstances suggests you are unbalanced, Major," Zimin answered calmly. "My officers are witness to this. If you persist in these wild accusations, we will be forced to restrain you for your own good, Major."

Tchenko did not reply. He marched across the deck to where the first MiG had been fueled and readied to take off. The flight crew stood aside and allowed the KGB officer to climb up to the cockpit. One of Zimin's men started to chase after Tchenko, but the captain placed a hand to his elbow to hold him back.

"*Nyet,*" Zimin told him. "Don't try to stop Tchenko. He's obsessed. He might even open fire on us if we get in his way. Let him go. If he can reach Barracuda before the Americans and destroys it, this entire insane affair will be over. Then we can charge him with unauthorized use of the plane and, hopefully, compounded with the charges he'll face for the Spetsnaz disaster, the major will face just punishment when he returns to Moscow."

"What if the Americans are already there and he engages in combat with them?" the officer inquired. "Tchenko is demented enough to attack them."

The MiG roared to life and shot down the runway of the *Chekov*. It bolted into the sky like steel lightning. Zimin frowned as he watched the fighter rocket toward the Guatemalan coast.

"Get an observation plane in the air as quickly as possible," he announced. "One equipped with a long-range telescope mount. Tell him to use the camera. Whatever happens, we want documentation. If it's too embarrassing, we can always destroy the film later. What I want to know is whether or not any American aircraft are in the area where Barracuda went down."

"And if they are?" the officer asked.

"Then we'll radio the American aircraft carrier and tell them the truth," the captain replied.

"The truth?" his officer asked with a frown.

"That a madman has stolen one of our fighter jets," Zimin said with a shrug.

26

Gary Manning completed wrapping the last length of primacord around the base of a tree trunk and placed a small amount of plastic explosives against the bark, packed tightly around the thick black cord. The Canadian demolitions expert jogged to the rear of Barracuda and joined Katz and Encizo. David Mc-Carter was busy squeezing into Lieutenant Roskov's flight suit. It was a tight fit, and the Briton had to remove the life preserver and G-suit bladder in order to be able to move in the suit. At least the helmet fit well. It was a single visor type. Double visors are only for flyers who have to worry about getting hit by birds. Barracuda was designed to fly higher than that.

"At least the ground doesn't seem too muddy," Encizo commented. "Still, this plane is awfully heavy."

The Cuban stared at Barracuda. The MiG looked like a great metal bird of prey. Like the MiG-27, and many other fighters made by the West as well as by the Soviet Union, Barracuda had "swing-wings," which folded while on the ground to make it easier for parking in limited space and taxiing when conditions were less than favorable for a full wingspan. Conditions seemed about as unfavorable as they could get right about then.

"Here we go," Manning announced. "Let's hope this works."

He pressed the plunger to an electrical squib wired to the primacord. Strands of the thick, explosive cords extended through the rain forest, wrapped around tree trunk after tree trunk like an enormous garland. The primacord burst and one by one detonated the RDX charges placed at each trunk. Trees crashed to the ground. Some toppled out of the path of the MiG. A few failed to oblige and landed across the improvised runway.

"Oh, hell," Manning muttered as he examined the clearing. The majority of the trees had been chopped out of the way by the expertly placed explosives. It was a remarkable job, yet Manning was less than satisfied. "Hang on. I'll see if I can take care of these stubborn logs."

The demolitions pro jogged to the trees still in the way and set more charges. Encizo glanced under the nearest wing of Barracuda and saw the nose of a pointed white missile. There were also two big torpedolike objects stored under the wing, one nearly twice the size of the other. He whistled softly.

"This thing is really packing an arsenal," the Cuban remarked.

"Bloody right," McCarter replied. "It has two tactical ASMs. Heat-seeking missiles. It also has both FAB-250 and 500 series bombs. The little ones are 551 pounds, and the big 500 models weigh more than a thousand. The multibarrel gun is 23 mm. This Barracuda definitely has teeth. It can kick some arse."

"Not this time," Katz stated. "I already noticed the bombs and missiles. There's Russian printing on them that explains these devices are not live."

"The rest of us don't read Russian," McCarter muttered. "You mean these are all dummy bombs and missiles? I hate flying a plane without real weapons."

"Dummies?" Encizo said with a frown. "Well, I guess Roskov was just flying a test with the Barracuda. There wasn't any reason he'd have live bombs or ammo."

"But these are authentic as far as size and weight is concerned," Katz stated. "On one bomb is printed '500kg'. That's a thousand one hundred and two pounds. Maybe you should dump some of this excess weight before you try to fly out of here."

"I might need that weight to keep this bird steady," McCarter explained. "If I swerve, I'll go off the path and into the trees. That'll be a bleeding mess, and we'll have to destroy her. That'd be a pity, because this is a beauty. If I have trouble with lift-off, I'll drop some of this excess gear."

Manning returned from planting the charges. The explosions erupted, and the logs in the proposed runway burst into splinters and left a path almost two hundred yards long and and more than one hundred feet wide. The Canadian nodded with satisfaction. Encizo clapped a hand on his shoulder.

"That's incredible, Gary," the Cuban told him. "I doubt there's another demolitions man in the world who could do better. Probably not more than half a dozen who could do it as well."

"You did your job, mate," McCarter told the Canadian. "Time for me to do mine."

The Briton climbed onto Barracuda and slid into the cockpit. Katz received a message on a field radio, set to the frequency used by Dragon Slayer. He listened briefly and spoke into the handset, then turned to his teammates.

"They delivered Roskov to the hospital personnel aboard *Anaconda*," Katz announced. "Looks like he'll be fine. Jack has refueled Dragon Slayer and will be heading out here to pick us up now."

"You blokes wait here for him," McCarter called out as he slapped down the visor to his helmet. "If all goes well, I'll beat you all getting to *Anaconda*. Stand clear. I'm about to move this bird."

The others backed away from Barracuda as McCarter closed the hatch. Encizo and Manning picked up fire extinguishers and waited tensely. The turbo engines came to life with a fury of sound, and the MiG rolled forward. The whine of the engines grew louder as the Barracuda accelerated and rushed along the improvised path. The wings began to extend, and flame streaked the afterburners as the fighter shot forward and the landing gear rose from the ground.

Surrounding trees caught fire from the afterburner burst. The MiG reached the end of the runway and rose swiftly. The landing gear brushed the top branches of a tree, but the plane continued to ascend and finally cleared the rain forest. Manning and Encizo rushed to the flaming trees and sprayed foam from the extinguishers to put out the blaze.

Katz watched the MiG sail into the sky. He sighed with relief. "That was a bit too close," the Israeli remarked.

"Yeah," Manning agreed. He stared at Barracuda and shook his head. "That crazy Cockney is one hell of a pilot."

"I know," Encizo commented. "I was with him when he landed that Beech on a damn driveway. Broke off both wings, but damned if he didn't land it."

"I remember when he crash-landed a helicopter when we had that mission in the Bahamas," Manning said with a groan. "I sure hope he can manage a more graceful landing when he reaches the *Anaconda*. It's gonna be embarrassing if he takes out a couple Harriers and an F-14 or two."

"Well," Katz began, "I'd say Barracuda is in good hands now and all we have to do is wait for Jack to come get us...."

The roar of another turbojet engine suddenly echoed from above the Pacific. They looked up and saw another aircraft in the distance. It was a MiG fighter, almost identical to Barracuda in design and size.

"What the hell is that thing doing?" Manning asked in astonishment.

"It's not here to do any sky writing," Encizo said grimly.

"It's another MiG," Manning stated as he raised a pair of binoculars and got a better look at the craft to confirm what they already feared. "The Russians wouldn't be crazy enough to attack Barracuda, would they?"

Katz replied, "We would have destroyed it if we couldn't get Barracuda airborne. The Soviets don't want us to have the new MiG or Roskov. They probably assume Roskov is piloting the Barracuda. This gives them a chance to kill two figurative birds with one ASM stone.''

''But they only sent one plane after Barracuda,'' Encizo observed. ''Wouldn't they send a whole squadron? I know Barracuda isn't armed, but still....''

''What do you mean it isn't armed?'' Manning demanded. ''Are you saying McCarter is up there about to be attacked and he can't fight back?''

''No live ammo and only dummy bombs and missiles,'' Katz said solemnly as he reached for the radio.

''Jack's headed back with Dragon Slayer,'' Encizo reminded them. ''Maybe that will even the odds.''

''Dragon Slayer is a gunship,'' Katz answered, the handset to the radio in his fist. ''It's not designed for the same altitudes or speed as a fighter jet. I'm going to try to contact *Anaconda* and see if Garner can get some fighters in the air pronto.''

''David could be blown out of the sky before they even get ready to taxi the runway on the carrier,'' Manning remarked, and shook his head.

''I know!'' Katz replied, more sharply than he intended. Then he lowered his voice and repeated, ''I know, but right now there's nothing else we can do.''

27

David McCarter liked Barracuda. The Soviet-made fighter handled beautifully. It was a better machine than the old MiG-25 he had flown in the past, and the instruments were almost identical to those of the MiG-27 simulators he had trained with. Although he could not read the Cyrillic writing on the controls, the British ace knew what they were and how they functioned even if he didn't know what they were called in Russian.

As always, McCarter was delighted to be flying a well-made aircraft. The sense of freedom and hurtling through the sky with total control of speed and direction never failed to fill him with satisfaction and exhilaration. The clear blue firmament stretched out before him like an invitation to race the plane at top speed, to open up and see what Barracuda could do.

The instruments registered 710 kmh. It was just cruising speed for the fighter. McCarter knew the MiG-27 could could reach Mach 1.6—almost twice the speed of sound. He was sorely tempted to see whether Barracuda could surpass that. The F-14 Phantom and the Tomcat could beat that Mach number. Yet the Briton wasn't certain how long the fuel supply would last, and he had ditched the drop tank when he got over the Pacific to increase altitude. After he did it, McCarter wished he had dropped the dummy bombs instead. The drop tank was eight hundred liters and he would have dumped more weight and retained fuel by getting rid of the nonexplosive bombs. Force of habit had caused him to hang on to the weapons even when he realized they were virtually useless.

Perhaps, if he could get permission from the skipper of the USS *Anaconda* to spend a few extra minutes testing Barracuda, he would not have to rush to the aircraft carrier to deliver the Russian fighter. He attached the oxygen mask with built-in mike across his lower face and reached for the radio control. Barracuda was equipped with VHF/UHF as well as RSIU antennae. He ought to be able to establish radio contact with *Anaconda*.

Suddenly a warning light appeared on the radar screen. Barracuda had radar scanners built into the radome. McCarter looked up at the radar screen and saw a blip approaching his position. It was moving in fast. Very fast.

"What the hell?" the Briton muttered as he peered through the windscreen and saw the plane coming up to his position.

It was a MiG-27 and appeared to be alone. A split second after McCarter identified the plane, the fighter opened fire with its 23 mm gun. The Briton cursed into his oxygen mask and accelerated. The enemy had opened fire more than eight hundred yards from Barracuda. Too far away for accuracy. The 23 mm rounds fell short of their target. Whoever the pilot was, the son of a Soviet bitch was not experienced in air combat. He had attempted a rather clumsy head-on gun attack and triggered too soon. However, regardless of the MiG-27 pilot's lack of ability, he was flying a plane with weaponry and McCarter was not.

The Briton pulled up swiftly and climbed higher as the enemy craft gave chase. McCarter felt the pressure of the sudden acceleration and saw the sky blur past the windscreen. He glanced at the radar screen to see the MiG was still on his tail. The Phoenix pilot pointed the nose of the Barracuda straight up and turned sharply to fly upside down and swoop around in a smooth "rollaway."

The Soviet pilot fired the gun again. Rounds clipped the tail fins of Barracuda as McCarter completed the maneuver. His opponent swung to the left to try to cut him off. The Briton anticipated the maneuver and continued the roll to swoop low beneath the path of the MiG. The enemy craft sped into a fast circle to try to get Barracuda in its sights once more. McCarter tracked the Soviet fighter and rose swiftly to come up in front of the MiG-27 as it began to complete the turn.

McCarter grabbed the gun control and pressed the trigger by instinct. The multibarrel gun mounted at the underside of Barracuda's nose fired a short burst of blank 23 mm ammo. The Briton growled at himself for this useless gesture, but he was surprised to see the MiG-27 suddenly break and retreat instead of seizing the opportunity to respond to Barracuda's impotent assault with an effective counterattack with live ammo.

MAJOR TCHENKO HISSED with anger as he swung the MiG-27 around to try to recover from his retreat.

When Barracuda opened fire, the KGB man immediately fled. The sight of the flames spitting from the other plane's gun had prompted him to react as if Barracuda was equipped with live ammunition. Still angry, Tchenko opened fire with his 23 mm blaster as Barracuda performed a fast break and suddenly made an unexpected sharp turn in the direction of the attack. McCarter lifted his craft higher, and Tchenko's hastily aimed salvo tore into the clouds without even nicking the paint on Barracuda.

The KGB agent struggled to control his rage. Roskov—or whoever piloted Barracuda—was clearly a superior flyer, and Tchenko had to grudgingly acknowledge that. Nonetheless, Tchenko's MiG was fully armed and Barracuda was not. Regardless of how clever and evasive the other pilot might be, all Tchenko needed was one clear shot to bring him down.

He had used the 23 mm gun thus far, hoping he might be able to damage Barracuda enough to force it to land at sea without having to destroy the valuable advanced fighter jet. Tchenko had wanted to try to salvage Barracuda if possible and perhaps even recapture Roskov. The longer Barracuda managed to prolong the air battle, the more likely that the American aircraft carrier would send a squadron of fighters to rescue the renegade MiG. Reluctantly Tchenko realized he would have to destroy Barracuda... unless he could convince Roskov to surrender.

Tchenko grabbed the handset to his radio and keyed the frequency last known to be used by Barracuda. He snapped orders in rapid-fire Russian into the mask mike. The KGB major identified himself and warned Lieutenant Roskov to return to the *Chekov* immediately or he would be forced to destroy Barracuda.

"I can't understand a bloody word you said," a voice with a British accent replied in gruff English. "Get off the line. I'm trying to call somebody else."

"Who are you?" Tchenko demanded. Like many field-grade KGB officers in the service of the Foreign Operations Directorate, he spoke fluent English. "What are you doing with that fighter jet? It is property of Union of Soviet Socialist Republics. You have no right to it."

"So get a lawyer and I'll see you in court," McCarter's voice replied.

"I do not need a court or judges, Englishman," the KGB agent stated. "I am prepared to carry out your sentence and act as executioner."

"You haven't done too well so far," McCarter answered with a mocking chuckle. "Where did you learn to fly? Mail-order pilot courses?"

"You tell jokes?" Tchenko sputtered. "Do you find the idea of your own death amusing? Barracuda is not armed. You may evade me for the moment, but eventually I will hit you and destroy the plane and you with it. I am giving you a chance to surrender this stolen property of the Soviet Union and live to return to your country."

Tchenko wondered why a Briton was flying the plane. Probably an expert pilot hired by the Americans, he guessed. Even as the KGB agent spoke on the radio, he continued to try to track his plane and hoped to catch the pilot off guard. The scheme was not working. Barracuda continued to soar about the sky in an evasive and unpredictable pattern. The major was having enough trouble just keeping up with his quarry.

"I'm really impressed by your offer," McCarter told the Russian, "but I'm afraid I can't accept. You're wrong about Barracuda being unarmed, by the way. You blokes out to check on the people who lead up these MiGs. Somebody accidentally put one real ASM on board. Everything else is dummy weaponry, but I do have one genuine heat-seeking missile. If you don't back off, I'll have to use it."

Tchenko was silent for a moment and then said, "You are lying."

"You think so?" McCarter inquired. "Well, you're about to find out."

The Briton switched off his radio and thought, *I'm lying like a Persian rug.* He did not expect the bluff to work, but the pilot of the MiG-27 did not seem to have much air combat experience. Maybe he would back off from the threat as he had retreated when McCarter fired the blank 23 mm rounds.

The enemy fighter tried a cut-off maneuver again and fired a salvo at Barracuda. The burst seemed to be aimed at a wing in an effort to cripple the plane. McCarter descended swiftly, but heard at least one round smash into the wing tip. Fluid spit from the damaged portion. The round must have hit the hydraulic actuator, McCarter thought. Not good, but it could have been a lot worse.

Tchenko swooped down after Barracuda and prepared to unleash his ASMs. The heat-seeking missiles would home right into the after burners at the rear of

Barracuda. There was no way the cunning British pilot could escape this time.

Suddenly McCarter executed another break and
swerved across the path of the MiG. Tchenko held his
fire. Barracuda was suddenly too close. If he used the
missiles, the explosion would destroy the quarry, but
would also risk blasting the KGB man and his plane
out of the sky, as well. He swung away from Barracuda and tried to get enough distance to use the ASMs.
Barracuda rose high and sailed in front of the MiG-27
once more.

Tchenko was furious and frustrated. He descended
to swoop low, get under Barracuda and fire the missiles. The heat-seekers would rise to the target and nail
the enemy, attracted by the burners. The KGB man
smiled as he looked up through the canopy to see the
underbelly of Barracuda perhaps one hundred twenty
yards above. The Briton appeared to have slowed the
fighter a bit and did not seem in a hurry to move. The
cocky pilot was not as clever as he thought himself to
be, Tchenko thought as he prepared to trigger the
ASMs.

McCarter released the bombs. The big FAB-500 series dropped faster than the smaller, less heavy FAB-
250s. Tchenko saw the huge dummy bombs descend
and cast a shadow across the canopy. Too late he
realized the bombs were realistic in one respect. Each
FAB-500 weighed more than a thousand pounds.

One dummy bomb crashed into the canopy. It
struck with tremendous force from the long drop. The
canopy shattered on impact, and the nonexplosive

weight smashed Tchenko as he sat helplessly inside the cockpit.

The MiG-27 swung out of control. McCarter watched the fighter plunge nose-first into the Pacific. It did not explode, but sliced through the surface like a steel eagle diving for fish. The plane submerged swiftly and carried Major Tchenko to a watery grave. The Briton sighed with relief and adjusted the radio to search for *Anaconda*'s frequency. When he found it, the Phoenix warrior announced that he was headed home.

WHEN DRAGON SLAYER RETURNED from the Guatemalan shores with Katz, Manning and Encizo aboard, Barracuda was already on the runway of the USS *Anaconda*. The Navy crew were crowding around excitedly and examining the new Soviet fighter. David McCarter and Calvin James waited for their teammates to emerge from the gunship. The other members of Phoenix Force climbed from the helicopter, glad to be reunited at last.

"We caught part of your air show," Encizo told McCarter. "Pretty impressive flying."

"I thought so myself," the Briton replied with a grin.

"How's Roskov?" Katz inquired, directing the question to James.

"He's gonna be fine," the black commando assured him. "Want to go to the hospital wing and see him? He's been asking about you guys. He was worried you wouldn't make it back."

"We made it," Manning declared as he glanced at Barracuda. He was glad they managed to get the plane as well as the pilot, but he really did not want to look at it until more time had passed. "Let's go tell Roskov it's official. He's on his way to America."

DON PENDLETON's

MACK BOLAN ®

Backlash

Mack Bolan kicks open a hornet's nest when he discovers a Nicaraguan power monger has been running drugs off the coast of Miami to finance an overthrow of the Sandinista regime...and has had a lot of help from the CIA.

Now the Company wants out and calls on the one man who can salvage this operation gone haywire...THE EXECUTIONER!

Phoenix Force—bonded in secrecy to avenge the acts of terrorists everywhere

SEARCH AND DESTROY $3.95 ☐

American "killer" mercenaries are involved in a KGB plot to overthrow the government of a South Pacific island. The American President, anxious to preserve his country's image and not disturb the precarious position of the island nation's government, sends in the experts—Phoenix Force—to prevent a coup.

FIRE STORM $3.95 ☐

An international peace conference turns into open warfare when terrorists kidnap the American President and the premier of the USSR at a summit meeting. As a last desperate measure Phoenix Force is brought in—for if demands are not met, a plutonium core device is set to explode.

Total Amount	$ _____
Plus 75¢ Postage	_____.75
Payment enclosed	$ _____

SPF-A

TAKE 'EM NOW

FOLDING SUNGLASSES
FROM GOLD EAGLE

Mean up your act with these tough, street-smart shades. Practical, too, because they fold 3 times into a handy, zip-up polyurethane pouch that fits neatly into your pocket. Rugged metal frame. Scratch-resistant acrylic lenses. Best of all, they can be yours for only $6.99.
MAIL YOUR ORDER TODAY.

Send your name, address, and zip code, along with a check or money order for just $6.99 + .75¢ for postage and handling (for a total of $7.74) payable to Gold Eagle Reader Service. (New York and Iowa residents please add applicable sales tax.)

Remove from pouch

unfold once

unfold twice

and they're ready to wear

GES-1A

GOLD EAGLE

Gold Eagle Reader Service
901 Fuhrmann Blvd.
P.O. Box 1396
Buffalo, N.Y. 14240-1396

Offer not available in Canada.

**Able Team battles a Vietnamese drug network
in Southern California.**

SUPER ABLE TEAM #2

HOSTILE FIRE

DICK STIVERS

A South Vietnamese heroin network, so powerful during the
Vietnam War, is still intact, and this time they're doing business in
the U.S. The Black Ghosts, led by a former VC general, are growing
strong in Southern California and for good reason—they have special CIA training.

It's a situation that's making Able Team see red—and they're making it their mission to stop the communist presence from infil-
trating California.